And he didn't know what he meant to do with this woman—he didn't know how to make her his revenge when he couldn't seem to make her do anything—but he couldn't take *this* any longer. He couldn't stand it.

"I'm not empty inside," Chase blurted out, gravel and steel in his voice, and she jerked in her seat as if he'd smacked her. He hated himself as if he really had.

"What?"

But he was already crossing the room. He was already right there, looming above her, so obviously brutal and dangerous, and yet she still gazed up at him in a kind of wonder. Like she saw all the things in him he'd stopped wishing were there a long, long time ago.

Like she was as much a fool as he was.

"It's much worse than empty in here," he gritted out. "It's murderous dark, vicious and wrong, and there's no changing it. You should have run away from me when I gave you the chance, Zara. You should have understood that it was a gift, and I don't know that I'll hand you another one."

VOWS OF CONVENIENCE

Bound by duty!

The Whitaker name was once synonymous with power, wealth and control. But with the family business facing certain ruin, and its reputation turning into dust, the Whitaker siblings need to make the ultimate sacrifice to safeguard their futures…

HIS FOR A PRICE

Following the death of Mattie Whitaker's father, a merger with Greek tycoon Nicodemus Stathis's company will go a long way towards fixing her problem—but Nicodemus's help comes at a price…

October 2014

HIS FOR REVENGE

Chase Whitaker is playing his own dark game of revenge against Zara Elliot's father, the chairman of his board. He plans to replace him— but he has no defences against Zara's unstudied charm and natural beauty…

December 2014

HIS FOR REVENGE

BY
CAITLIN CREWS

First published in Great Britain 2014
by Mills & Boon, an imprint of Harlequin (UK) Limited,
Eton House, 18-24 Paradise Road, Richmond, Surrey, TW9 1SR

© 2014 Caitlin Crews

ISBN: 978-0-263-24342-0

Harlequin (UK) Limited's policy is to use papers that are natural,
renewable and recyclable products and made from wood grown in
sustainable forests. The
to the legal environmen

Printed and bound in G
by CPI Antony Rowe,

Caitlin Crews discovered her first romance novel at the age of twelve. It involved swashbuckling pirates, grand adventures, a heroine with rustling skirts and a mind of her own, and a seriously mouth-watering and masterful hero. The book (the title of which remains lost in the mists of time) made a serious impression. Caitlin was immediately smitten with romances and romance heroes, to the detriment of her middle school social life. And so began her life-long love affair with romance novels, many of which she insists on keeping near her at all times.

Caitlin has made her home in places as far-flung as York, England, and Atlanta, Georgia. She was raised near New York City, and fell in love with London on her first visit when she was a teenager. She has backpacked in Zimbabwe, been on safari in Botswana, and visited tiny villages in Namibia. She has, while visiting the place in question, declared her intention to live in Prague, Dublin, Paris, Athens, Nice, the Greek Islands, Rome, Venice, and/ or any of the Hawaiian islands. Writing about exotic places seems like the next best thing to moving there.

She currently lives in California, with her animator/comic book artist husband and their menagerie of ridiculous animals.

Recent titles by the same author:

HIS FOR A PRICE *(Vows of Convenience)*
UNDONE BY THE SULTAN'S TOUCH
A SCANDAL IN THE HEADLINES
  (Sicily's Corretti Dynasty)
A ROYAL WITHOUT RULES *(Royal & Ruthless)*

Welcome to the world, Baby Haslam!

CHAPTER ONE

ZARA ELLIOTT WAS halfway down the aisle of the white-steepled First Congregational Church she'd always thought was a touch too smug for its own good—taking up a whole block on the town green in the center of the sweetly manicured, white clapboard village that her family had lived in since the days of the first Connecticut Colony way back in the 1630s—before the sheer insanity of what she was doing really hit her.

She felt her knees wobble alarmingly beneath her, somewhere underneath all that billowing white fabric that was draped around her and made her look like a lumbering wedding cake, and she almost stopped right there. In front of the hundreds of witnesses her father had decided it was necessary to invite to this circus show.

"Don't you dare stop now," her father hissed at her, the genial smile he used in public never dimming in the slightest as his wiry body tensed beside her. "I'll drag you up this aisle if I have to, Zara, but I won't be pleased."

This constituted about as much paternal love and support as she could expect from Amos Elliott, who collected money and power the way other fathers collected stamps, and Zara had never been any good at standing up to him anyway.

That had always been her sister Ariella's department.

Which was how this was happening in the first place,

Zara reminded herself as she dutifully kept moving. Then she had to order herself not to think about her older sister, because the dress might be a preposterous monstrosity of filmy white material, but it was also much—*much*—too tight. Ariella was at least three inches taller than Zara and had the breasts of a preteen boy, all the better to swan about in bikinis and gravity-defying garments as she pleased. And if Zara let herself get furious, as she would if she thought about any of this too hard, she would pop right out of this secondhand dress that didn't fit her at all, right here in the middle of the church her ancestors had helped build centuries ago.

It would serve her father right, she thought grimly, but it wouldn't be worth the price she'd have to pay. And anyway, she was doing this for her late grandmother, who had earnestly believed that Zara should give her father another chance and had made Zara promise to her on her deathbed last summer that Zara would—but had left Zara her cottage on Long Island Sound just in case that chance didn't go well.

She concentrated on the infamous Chase Whitaker—*her groom*—instead, as he stood there at the front of the church with his back to her approach. He looked as if he was drawing out the romantic suspense when Zara knew he was much more likely to be concealing his own fury at this wedding he'd made perfectly clear he didn't want. This wedding that her conniving father had pushed him into in the months since Chase's own larger-than-life father had died unexpectedly, leaving Amos a distinct weakness in the power structure of Whitaker Industries that he, as chairman of its board of directors, could exploit.

This wedding that Chase would have been opposed to even if Zara had been who she was supposed to be: Ariella, who, in typical Ariella fashion, hadn't bothered to turn up this morning.

Zara had always prided herself on her practicality, a vastly underused virtue in the Elliott family, but she had to admit that there was a part of her that took in the sight of her waiting groom's broad, finely carved shoulders and that delicious height he wore so easily and wondered what it would be like if this was real. If she wasn't a last-minute substitute for the beauty of the family, who had once been breathlessly described in Zara's hearing as *the jewel in the Elliott crown.* If a man like Chase Whitaker—worshipped the world over for his dark blue eyes, that thick dark hair and that devastatingly athletic body of his that made women into red-faced, swooning idiots at the very sight of it, to say nothing of that crisp, delicious British accent he wielded with such charm—really was waiting for *her* at the end of a church aisle.

If, if, if, she scolded herself derisively. *You're an idiot yourself.*

No one, it went without saying, had ever described Zara as a gemstone of any kind. Though her much-beloved grandmother had called her *a brick* once or twice before she'd died last summer, in that tone women of Grams's exalted social status had only ever used to refer to the girls they considered *handsome enough* and even *dependable* instead of anything like *pretty.*

"You're so dependable," Ariella had said two days ago, the way she always did, with that little smile and that arch tone that Zara had been choosing to overlook for the better part of her twenty-six years. Ariella had been putting on her makeup for one of her prewedding events, an exercise which took her a rather remarkable amount of time in Zara's opinion. Not that she'd shared it. "I don't know how you can bear to do it all the time."

"Do I have a choice?" Zara had asked, with only the faintest touch of asperity, because the way Ariella had said *dependable* was anything but complimentary, unlike the way Grams had said it back when. "Are *you* planning to step up and be dependable at some point?"

Ariella had met Zara's gaze in the mirror, a bright red lipstick in one languid hand. She'd blinked as if amazed by the question.

"Why would I?" she'd asked after a moment, as light and breezy and dismissive as ever, though her expression had bordered on scornful. "You're so much better at it."

That had obviously been a statement of intent, Zara thought now, as she moved closer by the second to the man at the end of the aisle. Who wasn't waiting *for her.* Who, given a choice, wouldn't be there at all.

Zara was glad she was wearing the irksome, heavy veil that hid her away from view so that none of the assembled onlookers could see how foolish her imagination was, which would no doubt be written all over her face. The curse of a natural redhead, she thought balefully. Hair that she only wished was a mysterious shade of glamorous auburn instead of what it really was. *Red.* And the ridiculously sensitive skin to go along with it.

But then she stopped thinking about her skin and the things that might or might not be splashed across it in all those telling pinks and reds she couldn't control, because they reached the altar at last.

Amos boomed out his part of the archaic ceremony, announcing to all that he gave away *this woman* with perhaps an insulting amount of paternal eagerness. Then she was summarily handed over to Chase Whitaker, who had turned to face her but managed to convey the impression that he was still facing in the other direction. As if he was deeply bored. Or so mentally and emotionally removed from this absurd little exercise that he thought he *actually was* somewhere else entirely.

And Zara remained veiled, as if she was participating in an actual medieval wedding, because—as her father had reminded her no less than seventy-five times in the church lobby already—Chase needed to be legally bound to the family before this little bait and switch was discovered.

"How charming," Zara had said drily. "A fairy tale of a wedding, indeed."

Amos had eyed her with that flat, ugly look of his that she went to great lengths to avoid under normal circumstances. Not that waking up to find oneself in the middle of a farcical comedy that involved playing Switch the Arranged Bride with her absentee sister's unknowing and unwilling fiancé constituted anything like *normal.*

"You can save the smart remarks for your new husband, assuming you manage to pull this off," Amos had said coldly. As was his way, especially when talking to the daughter he'd called *a waste of Elliott genes* when she'd been a particularly ungainly and unattractive thirteen-year-old. "I'm sure he'll be more receptive to them than I am."

His expression had suggested he doubted that, and Zara had decided that one smart remark was more than enough. She'd busied herself with practicing her polite, "just married to a complete stranger" smile and pretending she was *perfectly fine* with the fact Ariella's dress didn't fit her at all.

Because what girl didn't dream of waddling up the aisle in a dress that had been cut down the back to allow her breasts to fit in it, then held together with a hastily sewn-up strip of lace she was afraid her stepmother had ripped off the bottom of the church's curtains?

Her soon-to-be husband took her hands now, his own large and warm and remarkably strong as they curled around hers. It made her feel oddly light-headed. Zara frowned at the perky boutonniere he wore in his lapel and tried not to think too much about the fact that her father clearly believed that if Chase got wind of the fact that it was *Zara* he was marrying, he'd run for the hills.

The arranged marriage part was no impediment, was the implication. Just the fact that it was to the less lovely, less fawned over, much less desirable Elliott sister.

It wasn't until she heard a strange sound that Zara realized she was grinding her teeth. She stopped before her father—glowering at her from the first pew—heard it and did something else to ensure this marriage happened according to his plans. Zara really didn't want to think about what that *something else* might entail. Switching one daughter for the next should really be at the outer limits of deceitful behavior, but this was Amos Elliott. He had no outer limits.

The priest droned on about fidelity and love, which verged on insulting under the circumstances. Zara lifted her frown to Chase Whitaker's famously beautiful profile, so masculine and attractive that it had graced any number of magazine covers in its time, and reminded herself that while this situation might be extreme, it wasn't anything new. Zara had always been the mousy sister, the dutiful sister. The sister who preferred books to parties and her grandmother's company to the carousing of a hundred idiotic peers. The quiet sister whose academic aspirations were always swept aside or outright ignored so that Ariella's various scandals and kaleidoscopic needs could be focused on instead. She'd always been the sister who could be relied upon to do all the unpleasant and responsible and often deadly boring things, so that Ariella could carry on with her "modeling" and her "acting" and whatever else it was she pretended to do that kept her flitting about the globe from one hot spot to the next, answerable to no one and spending their father's money as she pleased.

Stop thinking about Ariella, Zara ordered herself sharply, when Chase slanted a dark look her way, and she realized she was squeezing his hands too tightly.

She loosened her grip. And she absolutely did not allow herself to think about how warm his hands were, how strong and interestingly callused and yet elegant, holding hers in a manner that suggested his gentleness was only a veneer stretched thinly over a great power he didn't care to broadcast.

She definitely wasn't thinking about that.

Then it was her turn to speak, in as even a voice as she could manage, expecting Chase to tear off her veil and denounce her in front of the entire church when the priest slipped in her name instead of Ariella's, so quickly and quietly that she wasn't sure anyone even heard it. But he was too busy concentrating on something just to the right of her gaze—and again, she got the sense that he was ruthlessly holding himself in check. That doing so took every ounce of the obvious and considerable strength she could feel in him as he slipped the necessary rings onto her finger.

That, or he was as drunk as the faint scent of whiskey suggested he was, and was trying not to topple over.

He recited his own vows in a low, curt tone, that accent of his making each word seem that much more precise and beautiful, and when it was done, when Zara had slid his own ring into place, she felt dizzy with relief and something else she couldn't quite name. Was it really that simple? Had she really squeezed herself into an ill-fitting dress she couldn't zip up and a blindingly opaque veil and pretended to be her sister? For the singular purpose of trapping this poor man in one of her father's awful little plots, because this had seemed like *the chance* her adored Grams had advised her to give Amos before she wrote him off forever?

"You may kiss the bride," the priest intoned.

So it appeared that yes, she had.

Chase sighed. Then he paused, and for a moment, Zara thought he was going to decline. *Could* he decline? In front of all these people? In any possible way that wouldn't make her look unwanted and unattractive besides?

She didn't know if she wanted him to kiss her or not, if

she was honest. She didn't know which would be worse: being kissed by someone who didn't want to kiss her because he felt he had to do it, or *not* being kissed by him and thereby shamed in front of the entire congregation. But then he dealt with the situation by reaching over and flipping her veil back, exposing her face for the first time.

Zara held her breath, cringing slightly as she braced for an explosion of his temper. She could *feel* it, like the slap of an open fire much too close to her, and instinctively shut her eyes against it. She heard an echoing sort of gasp from the front of the church, where someone had finally noticed that glamorous Ariella Elliott was looking markedly shorter and rounder than usual today. But Chase Whitaker, her unwitting groom and now her husband, said nothing, despite the roar of all that fire.

So she braced herself, then opened her eyes and looked at him.

And for a moment everything disappeared.

Zara had seen a million pictures of this man. She'd seen him from across the relatively small rooms they'd both been in. But she'd never been this close to him. So nothing could possibly have prepared her for the wallop of those eyes of his. Dark blue, yes. But they were the color of twilight, moments before the stars appeared. The color of the sea, far out from a lonely shore. There was nothing safe or summery blue about them. There was a wildness about that color, a deep, aching thing that she felt in her like a restless wind.

And he was beautiful. Not merely handsome or attractive the way he appeared in photographs. Not ruggedly lovely in some stark, masculine way, like dangerous mountain peaks were pretty, though he was decidedly, inarguably male. He was simply *beautiful*. His cheekbones were a marvel. His hair was a rough black silk and his brows were a great, arched wickedness unto themselves. His wide mouth made her feel much too warm, even flat and expression-less as it was now. And those stunning, arresting eyes, the blue of lost things, of shattered dreams, tore through her.

It took her a moment to register that he was staring down at her, incredulous.

And—as she'd already figured out from that blast of temper that she could still feel butting up against her like a living, breathing thing—he was very, very angry.

Zara went to pull away, not in the least bit interested in remaining this close to *that much* temper, but her new husband forestalled any attempt to escape with the hand he curled around her neck. She imagined it looked tender from a distance. But she was much closer, and she could feel it for what it was. Threat. Menace.

Fury.

No matter that a bright hot burst of flame danced from the place he touched her and then throughout the rest of her. No matter that a shiver rocked through her or that she felt as if her whole body *woke up* at the sensation of that hot, male palm against the nape of her neck. Her lungs felt tight and her throat ached. Her knees felt wobbly again, but for a very different reason than they had before.

And then Chase Whitaker, who had been quite clear that he'd never wanted to marry anyone and wouldn't have chosen her if he had, bent his head and pressed his per-fect lips to hers.

It should have been awkward, Zara thought wildly. Even violating.

But instead, it was like her entire body simply...sizzled. Her lips felt seared through, and she felt herself flush what she knew would be a revealing, horrifying red. She felt that simple press of his lips everywhere. In her throat. In that ache between her breasts. In her suddenly too-tight nipples. In that hard knot in her belly, and worse, in the sudden molten heat below it. Chase lifted his head, his remarkable eyes darker than before, and she knew he saw all of that betraying color.

And worse, that he knew what it meant.

There was something taut and electric between them then, something that sparked in the air and then moved inside of her, setting off alarms and making her feel that she really might collapse in the first faint of her life, after all. Like the archaic, bartered bride she was impersonating today. *Maybe that would be a nice little vacation from all this*, a small voice inside her suggested, while everything else she was or ever had been drowned in those dark blue eyes of his.

And then he looked away and everything sped up.

There was applause, then organ music, then the murmuring of several hundred scandalized guests who'd finally caught on to the fact that Chase Whitaker, president and CEO of Whitaker Industries and one of the world's most beloved playboy heirs, had just wed the wrong Elliott daughter.

Zara found this as unbelievable as they did, she was certain, but she didn't have time to reflect on it. Chase was holding her by the arm—in a manner that made her feel rather more like a prisoner than a bride, and yet, somehow, more cherished than when Amos had done the same thing—and they were starting off down the aisle again. She saw her father's smug face as they strode past him. She saw her stepmother dabbing at her eyes, and thought that ditzy Melissa might in fact be the only person in the church who'd found the ceremony moving, bless her. She saw longtime neighbors and old family friends and the speculative expressions of a hundred strangers, but the only real thing was that hard arm that held her next to his impossibly lean and chiseled body.

And then there was silence. Chase marched them out of the church and down the steps into the searing, brutal cold of the December afternoon, then directly into the back of a waiting limousine.

"Home," he grated at the driver. "Now."

"The reception is actually here in the village, not wherever your home is," Zara said, because she was incapable of keeping her mouth shut.

Chase had thrown himself into the cushy leather seat beside her and when he turned that furious, incredulous gaze of his on her again, it was like being burned alive. She felt charred.

He stared at her. Moments passed, or maybe years. The car drove off from the church. The world could have exploded outside the window, for all she knew. There was nothing but that wild dark blue and the leftover heat where his mouth and his palm had touched her skin, like he'd branded that contact into her flesh.

Then the car jolted to a stop at a light, Chase blinked and looked forward again, and Zara decided she'd imagined that awestruck, spellbound, *on fire* feeling. It was the oddness of the situation, that was all. It was Ariella's ridiculous dress, cutting into her like a corset from hell, making it difficult to breathe. There was no reason at all to feel that despite everything, she'd never been more alive in her life than she was right now, in the back of a limousine headed God knew where with an angry, beautiful stranger.

"Oh, I'm sorry," she said, because they might as well make the best of it. It was what Grams would have done. "I don't think we've ever met." She smiled as politely as she could at this man, her brand-new husband, and stuck out her hand. "I'm Zara."

He was trapped in a nightmare, Chase thought, staring at that outstretched hand in stunned, outraged amazement. There was no other explanation. For any of this.

"I know who you are," he grated, and when he didn't

take her hand she merely dropped it back in her lap, looking wholly unperturbed. Exactly as she'd looked in the
church, when he'd been glaring at her fiercely enough to
burn holes through her.

Except for when you kissed her.

But Chase shoved that thought away, along with the
image of her flushing that intriguing shade of scarlet in
the wake of that kiss he still didn't know why he'd given
her, and scowled at his bride instead.

The truth was, while he'd recognized who she must
have been because she'd been ushered up the aisle by his
nemesis, he couldn't remember if they'd ever met before.
He wasn't sure he'd have known her name even if they
had, just as he wasn't sure why that made him feel something like ashamed. He had a vague memory of her in a
black dress that had fit her much better than the gown she
wore today, and a flash of red hair from across a table.
That was it.

Every other interaction he'd had with her family had
involved her pain-in-the-ass father and blonde, brittle Ariella, who was apparently even more useless than he'd already imagined she was. And his imagination had been
rather detailed in its low opinion of her.

"You tricked me," he said then, trying to gather his wits,
as he'd been noticeably unable to do for some time now.
Since Big Bart Whitaker had died six months ago, leaving him neck deep in this mess that got bigger and deeper
and *swampier* every bloody day. Since he'd had to give up
his life in London and come back to the States to take his
place as president and CEO of Whitaker Industries, where
he'd done nothing but clash with Amos Elliott—the driving opposing force on his board of directors and the bane
of his existence. And now his father-in-law, for his sins.
"I could have you up on fraud charges, to start."

Zara Elliott did not look alarmed by this possibility. She

was awash in masses and masses of a frothy, unflattering white fabric, like a foaming and possibly furious marshmallow had exploded from every side of her while her quietly aristocratic face remained serene. But her eyes— her eyes were a bright, warm gold. The color of late afternoons, of the sun dripping low on the winter horizon.

Where the hell had *that* come from? He must have had more whiskey for his breakfast than he'd thought.

"I'm three inches shorter than Ariella and at least two sizes larger," she said. "At a conservative estimate."

Her voice was smooth and warm, like honey. She sounded, if not happy, something like *content*. Chase didn't know how he recognized that note in her voice, given he'd never felt such a thing in his life.

So that was why it took him a moment to process what she'd said. "I don't follow."

"Was I tricking you or were you not paying very much attention, if you couldn't tell the difference the moment I set foot in that church?" She only smiled when he scowled at her. "It's a reasonable question. One we can ignore, if you like, but which a judge may dwell on in any hypothetical fraud trial."

"This hypothetical judge might well find himself more interested in the marriage license," Chase replied. "Which did not have your name on it when I grudgingly signed it."

Her smile only deepened. "My father imagined that might cause you some concern. He suggested I remind you that the license was obtained right here in this very county, where he's reigned supreme for decades now, like his father, uncles, grandfather and so on before him. He wanted me to put your mind at ease. That license will read the way it should before the end of the day, he's quite certain."

Chase muttered something filthy under his breath, which had no discernible effect on her composure. He leaned forward and rummaged around until he found the half-drunk bottle of whiskey in the bar cabinet and then he took a long swig of it, not bothering to use a glass. That sweet, obliterating fire rolled through him, but it was better than the numbness inside of him, so he ignored the scraping flames and took another hefty swig instead.

After a moment, he offered her the bottle. It only seemed polite, under the circumstances.

"No, thank you." Also polite. Scrupulously so.

"Do you drink?" He didn't know why he cared. He *didn't* care.

"I like wine, sometimes," she said, as if she was considering the matter in some depth as she spoke. "Red more than white. I'll admit that beer is a mystery to me. I think it tastes like old socks."

"This is whiskey. It doesn't taste of socks. It tastes of peat and fire and the scalding anticipation of regret."

"Tempting." Her soft mouth twitched slightly in the corners, and he decided the whiskey was going to his head, because he found that far more fascinating than he should have. He couldn't recall the last time a woman's naked mouth had seemed so *riveting*. He couldn't recall the last time he'd noticed a woman's mouth at all, save what it could do in the dark. "How much whiskey did you have before the ceremony?"

He eyed her for a moment, then eyed the bottle. "Half."

"Ah." She nodded. "I thought you might be drunk."

"Why aren't you?" he asked, not caring that the dark rasp in his voice gave away far too many of the things he needed to keep hidden.

"Sadly, that wasn't on the list of options I was given when I woke up this morning and was informed Ariella had flown the coop." Her impossibly golden eyes gleamed with something almost painful Chase didn't want to understand, but her voice was still perfectly cheerful. It didn't make any sense. "I had to fight for a single cup of coffee in all the panic and blame. Asking for something alcoholic would have started a war."

He felt something very much like *ashamed* again, and he didn't like it. It hadn't occurred to him that she might find this marriage as unlikely and unpleasant a prospect as he did, and he didn't know why something in him wanted to argue the point. Like it made any difference who wanted what. They were both stuck now, weren't they? Just as her father had intended.

And it didn't matter to him which Elliott sister was stuck with him in Amos's handiwork. It made no difference to his plans. No matter what Zara's mouth did to his peace of mind.

Chase decided he didn't particularly care for any of these thoughts and took another long pull from the whiskey bottle instead. Oblivion was the only place he truly enjoyed these days. He'd considered permanently relocating there, in fact. How hard would it be to lose himself entirely in this or that bottle?

But he never did it, no matter how many nights he'd tried. Because the fact remained: the only thing he had left of his father, of his parents and his family legacy, was Whitaker Industries. He couldn't let it fall entirely into Amos Elliott's greedy hands. He'd already compromised and merged companies with the man his father had considered a better son to him than Chase had ever been. He couldn't sell it now. He couldn't step aside.

He couldn't do anything but this.

Chase took another drink from the bottle, long and hard.

"Where is your sister?" he asked, with what he thought was remarkable calm, under the circumstances.

Those golden eyes cooled considerably. "That's an excellent question."

"But you don't know?" He let his gaze track over that face of hers, her pale skin blending into the white veil that

billowed around her, reminding him of a bird's plumage.
He found he was fascinated by the fact her voice remained
the same, so unassailably polite, no matter what her gaze
told him. Her mouth bothered him, he decided. It was too
full. Too soft and tempting. Especially when she smiled.
"That's your position?"

"Chase," she said, then hesitated. "Can I call you that?
Or do you require that your arranged brides address you
in a different way?"

He let out a short laugh, which shocked the hell out
him. "Chase is fine."

"Chase," she said again, more firmly, and he had the
strangest sensation then. Like this was a different time and
there truly was an intimacy to the use of proper names. Or
maybe it was just the way she said it; the way it sounded in
that mouth of hers. "If I knew where Ariella was, I wouldn't
have shoehorned myself into this dress and married you in
front of three hundred of my father's closest friends, neighbors and business associates." She smiled at him, though
those impossible eyes were shot through with temper then,
and he understood that was where the truth of this woman
was. Not in her practiced smiles or her remarkably cheery
voice, but in her eyes. Gold like the sunset and as honest.
"If I knew where she was I would have gone and found her
and dragged her to the church myself. She is, after all, the
Elliott sister who agreed to marry you. Not me."

He watched her mildly enough over his whiskey bottle,
and noted the precise moment she realized she'd devolved
into something like a rant. That telltale color stole over her
cheeks, and he watched it sweep over the rest of her, down
her neck and to parts hidden in all that explosive white.
He found he was fascinated anew.

"No offense taken," he said, forestalling the apology
he could see forming on her lips. "I didn't want to marry
either one of you. Your father demanded it."

"As a condition of his agreement to back you and your new COO, yes," she said. "Your new brother-in-law, if I'm not mistaken?"

"Nicodemus Stathis and I have merged our companies," Chase said, as thinly and emotionlessly as he could. "And our families, as seems to be going around this season. My sister tells me she's blissfully happy." He wondered if Zara could see what a lie that was, if that was what the slight tilt to her head meant. If she knew, somehow, how little he and his younger sister Mattie had talked at all in the long years since they'd lost their mother, much less lately. He shoved on. "Your father is the only remaining thorn in my side. You—this—is nothing more than a thorn-removal procedure."

That was perhaps a bit too harsh, the part of him that wasn't deep in a fire of whiskey reflected.

"No offense taken," she said, her voice as merry as his had been cool, though Chase wasn't certain he'd have apologized, if she'd given him the chance. Or that she wasn't offended, come to that. "I'm delighted to be of service."

"I know why Ariella was doing this—or why she said she was all right with it," Chase said then, bluntly. "She quite likes a hefty bank account and no commentary on how she empties it. Is that a family trait? Are you in this for the money?"

Did he only imagine that she stiffened? "I have my own money, thank you."

"You mean you have your father's." He toasted her with his bottle. "Don't we all."

"The only family money I have came from my grandmother, as a matter of fact, though I try not to touch it," she replied, still smiling, though that warm gold gaze of hers had iced over again, and Chase knew he should hate the fact he noticed. "My father felt that if I wouldn't follow his wishes to the letter, which involved significantly less school and a lot more friendly games of things like tennis to attract his friends' sons as potential boyfriends-slash-merger options, I shouldn't have access to any of his money."

"Your sister makes defying your father her chief form of entertainment," Chase said, focusing on that part of what she'd said instead of the rest, because *the rest* reminded him of the many steps he'd taken to make sure that, while his father might have employed him, Big Bart had never supported him. Not since the day he'd turned eighteen. And he didn't want that kind of common ground with this woman. "She told me so herself."

"Yes," Zara said calmly, her gaze steady on his. "But Ariella is beautiful. Her defiance lands her on the covers of magazines and the arms of wealthy men. My father may find her antics embarrassing, but he views those things as a certain kind of currency. In that respect, I'm broke."

Chase blinked. "I'm very wealthy," he pointed out. "In all forms of currency."

"I didn't marry you for your money," she said gently. "I married you because this way, I can always remind my father that I sacrificed myself for him on command. To a wealthy man he wanted to control. Talk about the kind of currency Amos Elliott appreciates." Her mouth shifted into that smile of hers that did things to him he didn't like or understand. "He isn't a very nice man. It's better to have leverage."

Chase felt caught in the endless gold of her eyes then, or perhaps it was the near-winter afternoon outside the window that seemed to be some kind of extension of them, the sun brilliant through the stark trees and already too close to the edge of night.

"Are you looking for a nice man, then?" he asked quietly. From somewhere inside himself he hardly recognized.

"It would be difficult for you to be a worse one than my

father," Zara replied in the same tone. "Unless it was your singular purpose in life and even the briefest Google search online makes it clear that you've had other things to do."

Was she being kind to him? Chase couldn't fathom it. It made something great and gaping hinge open inside of him, too near to all that darkness he knew better than to let out into the light. He knew better than to let anyone see it. He knew what they'd call him if they did. He called himself that and worse every day.

Monster. Murderer.

He had blood on his hands that he could never wash clean, and this woman with eyes like liquid gold and the softest mouth he'd ever touched was being *kind* to him. On the very day her vicious father had lashed them together in unholy matrimony.

"I sold my own sister into her marriage because it benefited the company. I sold myself today." His voice was colder than the December weather outside. Colder than what he kept locked inside. And all those things he hid away swelled up in him then. Those memories. Those terrible choices. The day he'd lost his mother on that South African road where he'd made the choice that defined him, the choice that he still couldn't live with all these years later. To say nothing of the truth about his relationship with the father he felt he still had to prove himself to, even now, when Big Bart Whitaker would never know the difference. "You'll want to be careful, Zara. I'll ruin you, too, if you let me."

She studied him for a moment, and then she smiled, and he didn't know how he knew that this one was real. Even if it felt like it drew blood.

"No need to worry about that," she said quietly. "I won't."

CHAPTER TWO

THE HOUSE WAS like something out of a Gothic novel.

Zara had to fight to conceal her shiver of recognition from the man who lounged beside her in the black mood he'd worn throughout the drive.

"Cold?" he asked. Chase's voice was polite on the surface, but his gaze was a wilderness of blue and almost liquid, somehow, with a kind of sharp heat that speared straight through her. And none of it friendly.

"Not at all," Zara said, though she was. "Your house isn't the most welcoming place, is it?"

Gothic, she thought again. She'd read significantly more Gothic novels than the average person and not only because she was writing a master's thesis on the topic. On some level she should have expected she'd find herself in the middle of one. It was the only thing her absurd wedding day had been missing.

"It's December." Chase's voice was as cold as his estate looked in the beam of the limousine's headlights. Barren and frozen as far as the eye could see. "Nothing in this part of the country is welcoming at this time of year."

But it was more than that. Or it was her imagination, Zara amended, which had always been as feverish as the rest of her was practical. The old stone manor rose like an apparition at the top of a long, winding drive through a thick and lonely winter forest of ghostly, stripped-bare trees and unfriendly pines coated with ice and the snowy remains of the last storm. Several inches of snow clung to the roof above the main part of the house, and each of its wings glittered with icicles at the gutters, though the sky above tonight was clear. Thick and almost too dark, but clear.

She tried to imagine the house festooned in spring blossoms or warmed by the summer sun, and failed. Miserably.

For the first time in her life, Zara questioned her addiction to Daphne du Maurier and Phyllis A. Whitney novels. They might have helped her through an awkward adolescence and paved the way toward what she hoped would become her life's work, but they had also made her entirely too susceptible to the dark possibilities lurking in a scary old mansion, a bridegroom she scarcely knew and whatever rattled around in the gloomy shadows of places like this.

"Are you sure you don't have any madwomen locked away in the attic?" she asked, appalled when her voice sounded more shaken than wry.

"Making me a convenient bigamist and you therefore free of this mess we're both stuck in?" he replied, smooth and deadly, and shocking Zara. She wouldn't have pegged him as a reader of *Jane Eyre*. Or a reader at all, come to that, when he could be off brooding beautifully somewhere instead. "I'm afraid not. My apologies."

Chase did not sound remotely sorry. Nor did he sound drunk, which Zara couldn't quite understand. She'd expected sloppiness when he'd continued to drink from that whiskey bottle throughout the drive, had braced herself for his unconsciousness and his snores. Instead, he simply seemed on edge.

More on edge, that was.

Maybe the place—and the man—was more welcoming in the daylight, Zara thought as diplomatically as possible as the car pulled up to the looming front entrance. Then again, it hardly mattered. She wasn't here to settle in and make a happy home for herself. She was here because Grams had wanted her to try. She was here because this proved, once and for all, that she was the good daughter. Surely this finally settled the matter. Surely her father would finally have to recognize—

"Come," her brand-new husband said from much too close beside her, his hand at her side and that disconcerting gaze burning into her as surely as that small contact did, and when she jerked her head around to stare back at him it was even worse. All that irrational, unmanageable fire. "I'd like to get out of these clothes, if you don't mind. And put this lamentable farce behind me as quickly as possible."

Zara couldn't keep herself from imagining beautiful Chase Whitaker without his clothes any more than she could stop herself from breathing her next breath. All that long, lean, smooth muscle. All that ruthlessly contained power—

Get a hold of yourself! she yelped inwardly.

And then she pretended she didn't see the way his eyes gleamed, like he could read her dirty mind.

Chase ushered her into the grand front hall of the sprawling stone mansion, adorned with art and tapestries and moldings so intricate they almost looked like some kind of architectural frosting, with what felt like more irritation than courtesy. He introduced her to his waiting housekeeper, Mrs. Calloway, without adjusting his stride and then marched Zara up the great stair to the second floor. Zara had the jumbled impression of graceful statues and priceless art, beautifully appointed rooms and long, gleaming hallways, all in a hectic blur as they moved swiftly past.

He didn't speak. And Zara found she couldn't. Not only was the house lifted from the pages of the books she studied, but now that she was *this close* to getting out of her horribly uncomfortable dress at last and, God willing, sinking into a very deep, very hot, restorative bath for about an hour or five, every single step that kept her from it was like sheer torture.

That and the fact that Chase was more than a little forbidding himself. It was that set way he held himself. Contained and furious, even as he prowled along beside her. It seemed particularly obvious in a place like this, all shadows and absence, empty rooms and echoing footsteps.

You're becoming hysterical.

When she felt like herself again, she was sure she'd stop thinking like this. *She was sure.* And then she'd fish her cell phone out of the bag she fervently hoped was in that limo and she would either listen to the host of apologetic messages Ariella should have left for her today, or, in their far more likely absence, call Ariella until her sister answered and explained this great big mess she'd made.

And then maybe all of this would feel a little bit less Gothic.

Particularly if she got out of this damned dress before it crippled her forever.

"Here," Chase grunted, pushing open a door.

Zara blinked. Her head spun and her heart began to race and her feet suddenly felt rooted to the floor. "Is this...?"

"Your rooms." He smirked. "Unless you planned to make this a more traditional marriage? I could no doubt be persuaded. I've certainly had enough whiskey to imagine anything is a good idea. My rooms are at the other end of this hall."

Zara thought she'd rather die than *persuade* him to do anything of the kind. Or anyone like him who would, she had no doubt, need nothing in the way of *persuasion* if she was lanky, lovely, effortlessly appealing Ariella.

Not that you want this man either way, she reminded

herself. Pointedly. She'd always been allergic to his type: basically, male versions of her sister. Younger versions of her father. Entitled and arrogant and no, thank you.

Despite that thing in her that felt like heat, only far more dangerous.

"Whiskey wears off," she said crisply. "And more to the point, I haven't had any." She brushed past him, determined to sleep in whatever the hell room this was, even if it was a cell and her only option was the floor. "This is perfect, thank you."

"Zara." She didn't want to stop walking, but she did, as if he could command her that easily. *You're tired*, she assured herself. *That's all*. "I'll be back later," he said, his voice dark and, yes, foreboding.

"For what? Persuasion? There won't be any. No matter when you come back."

He let out a noise that might have been a laugh, and the madness was that she felt it skim down the length of her spine like a long, lush sweep of his fingers.

There was no reason that she should have *felt* him the way she did then, like an imprint of fire, large and looming over her from behind, like he could cast a shadow and drown her in it all at once. And there was no reason that her body should react to him the way it did, jolting wide-awake and *hungry*, just like that.

"I'll be back," he said again, a low thread of sound, dark and rough, and she felt that, too. *Felt* it, like his hands against her skin.

She nodded. Acquiesced. It was that or succumb to panic entirely.

Zara waited until he closed the door behind her, then let out a long breath she hadn't realized she'd been holding. It came out in a kind of shudder, and she had to blink back all that overwhelming heat from her eyes.

Then she actually looked around her.

The bedroom suite was done in restrained blues accented by geometrical shapes etched in an elegant black, with a lit fireplace against one wall that was already crackling away and an inviting sofa and two chairs in front of it that begged for a book, a cozy throw blanket and a long, rainy afternoon's read. The bed was a cheerful four-poster affair, with quilts and blankets piled high and a multitude of deep, soft-looking pillows. It was a contented, happy sort of room, and it made all that Gothic fervor ease away, leaving Zara feeling overtired and foolish in its wake.

Her gaze snagged on the set of photographs on the mantel above the fireplace as she walked deeper into the room, all featuring pictures of a very tall, very recognizable black-haired girl, solemn dark eyes and an enigmatic almost-smile on her pretty face. *Mattie Whitaker.* Chase's infamous sister.

Zara read the tabloids, and not only when she was stuck in line at the supermarket. Mattie had been all over them recently for her "secret marriage" to "playboy Chase's greatest rival," which Zara didn't think could have been too terribly secret if there were all those pictures of Mattie and her harshly attractive husband gazing at each other in front of a glorious Greek backdrop. Just as Nicodemus Stathis couldn't possibly be the terrible rival the papers wanted him to be if Chase and he were working on a merger.

Shockingly, she told herself derisively, *the papers lie, as your entire life watching Ariella manipulate them to her benefit should have made you well aware.*

But it was Mattie Whitaker's bathroom she cared about then, not the marriage Chase had claimed he'd sold his sister into. Or what the tabloids might have made up about it.

"That," she said out loud as she headed for the far door across the bedroom, "will be something Mattie and I can bond over across the table at Christmas. Our delightful forced marriages, whether secret or not."

She lost her train of thought and let out a sigh of delight instead when she walked inside and found the bathtub of her dreams waiting for her, vast and deep enough for a group of people, placed before high windows that looked out into the silken night.

Bliss.

Zara turned on the tap greedily and dumped a capful of the foaming bath salts that sat on the tub's lip into the warm stream. Then she ripped that veil straight off her head, not caring that it tugged at her hair. That it *hurt*. It came off with a clatter of hairpins against the floor, and Zara moaned out loud in stark relief as she massaged her way over her abused scalp, pulling out the remaining pins and letting her hair fall free at last.

Now it was time to deal with that torturous dress. The water poured into the bath behind her as she tugged and pulled, twisting herself this way and that as she tried to free herself. It was far more difficult than it should have been—but Zara was desperate. She yanked even harder—

And then at last she heard a glorious tearing sound, the fabric finally gave—and she yanked it all off, kicking the tattered remains away as the dress fell to her feet in a voluminous cloud. At first, she hurt *more* than she had before. Her breasts ached, and she could see the angry lines the built-in corset had left all over them and her belly, red and pronounced because she had the kind of skin that showed every last mark like a neon billboard.

And because the dress had been made for her sister, who better resembled a starving gazelle and had needed that corset to create the illusion of the cleavage she didn't have rather than tamp down any existing breasts.

It was such a relief to be free of that hideous torture device that Zara's eyes filled with tears. But she refused to indulge them, not here in this too-Gothic mansion with the whiskey-pounding, possibly dangerous husband she'd never met before the ceremony. Not when she didn't know that she'd stop. Not when the wedding was only the latest in a long stream of things she could probably cry about, if she let herself.

Not here. Not tonight. Grams had maintained her stiff upper lip to the very last of her days. Zara could do the same with far less provocation.

She toed off the white ballet flats she'd worn all day— thank goodness she and Ariella wore the same size shoes and she hadn't had to make like one of Cinderella's unfortunate stepsisters and hack off a toe to fit into them—and shimmied out of the very bright, screaming red thong panties she'd worn beneath it all. The only thing in the whole, long, strange day that was hers.

Zara couldn't control the deep, atavistic sigh she let out when she slipped into the bath at last. The water was hot and the bubbles were high enough to feel decadent without being so high they became a problem. She piled her hair—wild and thick and incredibly unruly from a day in pins and scraped into submission beneath that veil— up on top of her head in a messy knot as she tried to picture glamorous, couture-draped Mattie Whitaker lounging in this bathtub the way she was now. Mattie Whitaker, who was a good deal like Ariella in Zara's mind—one of those effortless girls, all long, slender limbs; hot-and-cold-running boyfriends; and the ability to float through life without a single care.

Zara's life had been charmed in its own way yet was significantly less *gleaming*, despite the fact she, too, was an Elliott. She'd failed to look the part from birth and hadn't ever managed to act the part, either, despite the thousands of lectures Amos had delivered on the topic. Even when doing so would have been in her best interests.

Well. She'd acted the part today, hadn't she? She'd done

it. *I did what you asked, Grams*, she thought then. *I gave him one last chance to treat me differently.*

She shut her eyes and leaned back against the smooth porcelain, breathing in the jasmine-scented steam as she tried to expel all the tension of the day from her body. As she tried not to think about what had happened earlier in that church. Or what might happen later, because who knew what the expectations were in a situation this twisted? Or what she'd got herself into, marrying a man who was not only a total stranger, but who'd turned up to his own wedding half-drunk and entirely furious, and that had been before he'd seen the switch.

Zara didn't know how long she sat like that, the water cascading all around her, the jasmine heat like an embrace, soaking all the red marks from the vicious gown away into the ether and her headache along with it. She was lazily contemplating climbing out of the bath and investigating the possibility of dinner when she felt a shift in the air. Everything simply went taut, her skin felt too tight, and she reluctantly opened up her eyes.

To find Chase leaning there in the doorway, looking dark and disreputable, lethally dangerous in a way that made the back of her neck tingle, and nothing at all like drunk.

For a moment Zara stopped breathing. Her heart gave a mighty kick against her ribs and then jackrabbited into high gear. Her ears rang as if someone had screamed, and her throat ached as if she was that someone, but she knew she'd done nothing at all but stare back at the man who shouldn't have been there.

She needed to say something. She needed to *do* something. But he was so beautiful it hurt, even more so now that he'd changed out of his wedding suit and was something far more elemental in bare feet that defied the weather beneath a soft-looking button-down shirt he hadn't bothered to do up properly over a pair of jeans. And his dark blue eyes seemed wilder than before, remote and with that aching thing at once, like some kind of ruthless poetry. She didn't know what lodged in her chest then, only that it was much too sharp and alarmingly deep.

"Shouldn't you be passed out on a floor somewhere?" she asked, harsher than she'd meant to sound.

Maybe this was his version of drunken, idiotic behavior. She'd witnessed the bitter end of her parents' marriage over the course of too many drink-blurred nights, as they'd each got drunker and meaner. Ariella had sneaked out to escape it, while Zara had tried to hide from it in books where all the terrifying goings-on weren't usually real, in the end. She'd never seen the appeal of getting drunk since.

Though even that looked better than it should on Chase Whitaker.

"I'm not drunk," he growled at her. "Not nearly enough."

He shifted so he could prop one of those finely cut shoulders against the doorjamb, and she felt the way he looked at her like a touch. Hot and demanding. And she understood then, that what happened here would set the stage for the whole of their unconventional relationship, however long it lasted, and in whatever form. If he thought he could walk in on her like this, what else would he think he could do?

Zara had been raised on a steady diet of *no boundaries*. Her father was a tyrant. Her mother cared more about scoring her pound of flesh from him than her own daughters. The older sister she'd hero-worshipped when she was a kid turned nastier by the year. Ariella was on a crash course to becoming their father, a man who truly believed that he got to make whatever rules he felt like following that day by virtue of who he was and how much money and power he had.

Zara was fed up with *no boundaries*.

"You have to leave," she said, firm and direct. Unmistakable. "Now. I take my privacy very seriously."

"Are we not cleaved unto one?" Chase's tone was dark and there was something terrible in his gaze, mocking and harsh. "I'm sure I heard something about that earlier today."

"We are engaging in mutual thorn-removal, nothing more," she corrected him, using his phrase and not sure why it made that gaze of his get harsher. Wilder. Untamed in a way that made something deep in her belly coil tight. "And I may have married you, but I didn't agree to any kind of intimacy. I don't want any. That's not negotiable."

"Has anything about this been negotiable?" he asked, his voice almost idle, though Zara didn't believe it at all. Not when those eyes of his were on her, intent and arresting. "Because what I recall is your father parading your sister under my nose in a variety of questionable attire and telling me that he'd crush me if I didn't marry her."

Zara felt almost outside herself then, as if she was watching this interaction from a great distance. It was the way he'd said *questionable attire*, maybe, because it summoned Ariella as surely as if she was a genie in a bottle, and Zara wanted nothing more than to smash that bottle against the tile floor. If it had made any kind of sense, she would have thought what she felt was *hurt*. And something so close to *offended* it might as well have been the same thing.

"Is that what this is?" she asked with a coolness she didn't feel at all, not in any part of her, like that wilderness that he carried in him was catching. "You've been downgraded from the coveted main attraction to its much less interesting runner-up and you want to see the full extent of that downward spiral? Why didn't you say so?"

"I beg your pardon?"

Zara didn't let herself think it through. She slid both

her hands out to the high sides of the bath and then she stood up. Water coursed down her body and there was a howling sound inside her head, but she didn't take her gaze from Chase's.

Not for a second.

"This is it," she said, aware that her voice was shaking, and it wasn't with upset. It was more complicated than that. Challenge and disappointment and *fury*, and the fact that none of it made sense didn't make it any better. "Take a good look, because I'm not doing this again, and yes, it really is as bad as you fear. You married me, not Ariella. I'll never be any fashion designer's muse. I'll never be photographed in a bikini unless the goal is to shame me. No one would ever call me skinny and no one has ever claimed I was anything like beautiful. I'll never fast my way down to Ariella's weight and even if I did, even if I wanted to, it wouldn't matter. We're built completely differently."

For a moment—or a long, hard year or two—there was nothing but the sound of the water she stood in, still sloshing from how quickly she'd stood. And that pounding thing in her head that made her ears feel thick and her stomach churn.

Chase simply stared.

He was frozen in place, something she couldn't read at all stamped on his gorgeous face, making him look something other than simply beautiful. Something *more*. Something so dangerous and so intent, she felt it thud through her, hard. Then he blinked, slowly, and Zara understood that she cared a good deal more about what he might say next than she should.

Which meant she'd made a terrible mistake. As she so often did when she decided to act before she thought. Why could she never seem to learn that lesson?

"Yes," Chase scraped out into the close heat of the bathroom, in a hoarse voice that shivered over her like warm water but was much, much hotter, a match for that deep, dark blue of his gaze and as irrevocably scalding. "You bloody well are."

If she'd taken a sledgehammer to the side of his head, she couldn't have stunned him more.

She was so…pink. *So perfect.*

That was all Chase could think for long moments. She'd looked round and solid all draped in white as she'd been; stout and tented, like a gazebo. That's what he'd thought in the limousine, uncharitably. Perhaps *this* was his punishment.

Or, a sly voice inside of him, located rather further south than his brain, *she is your reward for all of this.*

It was hard to argue with that. She was a symphony of curves. Gorgeous, mouthwatering, stunning lushness, from the fine neck he could remember beneath his palm in the church in an almost alarmingly tactile manner to a pair of heavy, perfect breasts, plump and flushed from the damp heat yet marked by fine blue lines that reminded him how fair she was.

And nipples so pert they made his mouth actually ache to taste them. Chase was glad he'd happened to lean against the door, because he wasn't certain he could stand on his own.

Her waist was the kind of indentation that made him understand, profoundly, whole schools of art he'd never paid much attention to before, particularly with the breathtaking flare of her hips beneath, wide and welcoming and making that trim V between her legs all the more delectable.

He wanted to be there—*right there*—more than he could remember wanting anything. Ever.

All that and the riot of reds and coppers and strawberry blonds that she'd fastened atop her head somehow, the wet heat making tendrils into curls and spirals that framed her elegant face, making him as hard as a spike and incapable of thinking of anything for long moments but getting his hands in the mess of it, deep. Holding her still while he thrust himself between those perfectly formed thighs, plundered that astonishingly carnal mouth of hers, and happily lost what was left of his mind.

Chase was a product of his time, he understood then, and felt sorry for all the men his age. Like them, he'd always preferred longer, slimmer women by rote, preferably with the smooth leanness that spoke of countless years of deprivation. Women who wore clothes in ways that emphasized their narrow hips and the angular thrust of their collar and hip bones. Women who looked good in photographs, especially the kind that he was always finding himself in, splashed here and there in the harsh glare of the British press.

Women like Zara, he thought in a kind of daze as an ancient, primitive need he'd never felt before pounded through him, should never, ever be confined to anything as foolish as modern clothing. They should never be subjected to a dress like that monstrosity she'd worn today. They should never be contained in photographs that adored angles and punished soft curves. Not with bodies like this, like hers, that were made to be seen whole in all their primal glory. That were created purely to be worshipped.

She was branded into him now, he thought wildly, so red-hot and deep he might never see anything or anyone else again.

And he was so hard it hurt.

"Then we need never repeat this experience," she was saying, her voice a brittle slap against all that warm heat, and Chase was still knocked senseless. He couldn't follow what she was saying, not with his heart trying to kick its way out of his chest, so he stayed where he was and watched as she stepped out of the tub and yanked one of the towels from the nearby rack, wrapping that gorgeous body of hers away from view.

He wanted to protest. Loudly.

"You can go now," she said, her voice even more rigid than before, and when her gaze met his again, those miraculous eyes of hers were smoky with something bleak. "I trust it won't be necessary for any further object lessons tonight, will it?"

And Chase could think again then. With both his brains. More than that, he remembered himself and what he was doing, something he couldn't believe he'd lost track of for even a moment. He opted not to analyze that too closely. Not while the wife he didn't want was still within an easy arm's reach, her skin still pinkened and softened from her long soak, her warm golden eyes still shooting sparks—

He had to stop. He had to remember that whatever else she was, she was an Elliott. She might have proved herself far more interesting than her shallow, grasping, run-of-the-mill sister, to say nothing of *that body*, but she was still an Elliott.

Which meant there was only one way this could go.

"I appreciate the show," he said in a voice that made her jerk where she stood, as surely as if he'd hauled off and slapped her. Exactly as he'd planned, and yet Chase loathed himself at once—and he'd have thought he'd hit his maximum where that was concerned years before. *You always have somewhere lower to go, don't you?* He waited until the red blazed across her face, until her gaze turned stormy. "There's a private dining room on this floor, above the library. Follow the hall to the end and it will be the arched doorway in front of you. You've got ten minutes."

"And you will have to drag my dead body in there," she said, her voice stiff with a fury he could see all too plainly in her gaze. Fury and whatever that darker, harsher thing was. He told himself it wasn't his to know. That he didn't *want* to know. "As that is the only way I'll ever spend another moment in your company."

"Trust me, Zara," he said, his voice much too low and not nearly polite enough, things he didn't want to think about all over his face—or so he assumed from the way she stiffened in reaction, and not, he could see too plainly, because she was offended. "You don't want me to come back here and force the issue. You really don't."

CHAPTER THREE

CHASE WAITED FOR her in the small dining room, the place Big Bart had reserved for immediate family alone. There was a huge, formal dining room downstairs near the old-fashioned ballroom that now housed a grand piano Chase's mother had once played, and another medium-sized dining room that his father had used for smaller gatherings, but this one had always been off-limits. It was close. Intimate.

Exactly what Zara had indicated she didn't want.

His mouth twisted in derision, and Chase moved away from the window before he could look too closely at his own reflection there against the dark night beyond. He already knew what he'd see, and there was no point in it. There was nothing he could change now. It was done.

Going into that suite hadn't helped. It had only under-scored the scope of his own failures. He'd never spent much time in his sister's rooms, not even when he and Mattie had been small and far happier. Not even *before*.

Even now, all these years after she'd moved out and de-spite what she'd sacrificed two months ago for the fam-ily and the company by marrying Nicodemus Stathis, he couldn't think about his sister without losing another great chunk of himself in all that guilt. It cut too deep, left him nothing but gutted and useless. It had always seemed a kindness to simply keep his distance instead. To let her grow up without the dark weight of the secrets he carried. To let Mattie, at least, be free.

Not that it had worked.

I'm guessing you don't wake up every night of your life screaming then, Mattie had said the last time they'd spoken. She'd sounded raw. Unlike herself. He'd been as unable to face that as anything else. A coward down to his bones, but that hadn't been news. *Calling out for Mum again and again.*

Chase didn't wake up in the night, he thought now as he found himself by the window again, looking out toward the Hudson River at the low end of the property even though he couldn't see it with the dark December night pressing in on all sides. Nightmares would have been beside the point. He carried his ghosts around with him in the light.

He never forgot what he'd done.

And neither had his father.

Maybe that was why Big Bart Whitaker had left his empire in such disarray. It was so unlike him, after all. Chase had always been Bart's heir, and because of that he'd spent the past decade working his way up the ranks until he'd achieved the VP slot in the London office. He'd never minded that his future had been so mapped out for him. He'd enjoyed the challenge of proving he wasn't just his surname, but a capable businessman in his own right, no matter what the papers intimated. Everyone had always assumed that he'd move from London to the Whitaker Industries corporate headquarters in New York and transition into his eventual leadership of the company. That had always been the plan, except it had never been the right time, had it? Bart had always had other things to do first. Chase had always found a different reason to stay in London.

The truth, he acknowledged now, was that they'd been a good deal more comfortable with each other when there was a nice, wide ocean between them.

Maybe the fact that Bart had left Chase to fend for himself wasn't a mistake. Maybe Bart had thought that if Chase couldn't hold on to Whitaker Industries against the tiresome machinations of Amos Elliott or the cash flow issues that the merger with his brand-new brother-in-law would solve, he didn't deserve it.

And Chase couldn't find it in him to disagree.

He'd forgotten where he was, he realized when he heard a light step on the old floors behind him and scented the faintest hint of jasmine in the air.

"I don't understand what this is," Zara said from the doorway, her voice tight. But she'd still come on time, he noted. "I don't understand what you *want*."

Neither did he, and that should have alarmed him. It did. But it also occurred to him that the only time in the past six months—hell, in the past twenty years—that he'd actually forgotten about that lonely stretch of South African road and what he'd done there, what he'd become and what that had done to his family, was when Zara Elliott held his gaze and did her best to confound him, one way or another. In the bath, yes. God help him, *the bath*. But in the limo, as well.

He didn't want that to mean anything. But he couldn't seem to ignore it, either. And that spelled nothing but doom for them both.

Chase turned, slowly, and felt a deep, purely masculine regret lodge beneath his ribs when he saw she'd dressed. *Of course she had.* Black, stretchy pants that clung to those marvelous hips and her well-formed legs and what looked like a particularly soft sweater on top, a bit slouchy and roomy, so that her softly rounded shoulder peeked out when she moved. Her wild, glorious hair was combed through and fixed neatly at the nape of her neck, and he wanted the other Zara back. That powerful, compelling goddess creature he wanted to taste. Everywhere. With his teeth. That stunning woman he had the agony of knowing was *just there*, now hidden beneath clothes that couldn't possibly flatter her as much as no clothes at all did. Nothing could.

This was his bride. His *wife*. His wedding night, some darkness inside him reminded him.

Good lord, but he was still hard.

"This is our marriage," he told her, his voice a grating thing, harsh and a little too mean. He thought she'd flinch again, but her gleaming eyes only narrowed.

"This had better also be dinner," she said as crisply as if she was discussing the weather of a distant city. And as if she'd put on a sheet of armor beneath her clothes. "Or I may collapse from starvation. And while I might view that as a handy escape from all this excitement, I doubt that's what you have in mind."

"I've never had an arranged marriage before," he said grimly as she moved farther into the room with a wariness she made no effort to hide, then perched on the edge of the chair nearest the door. "Perhaps nightly collapses are but par for the course."

She eyed him. "Arranged marriages are really quite stable," she said after a moment. "Historically speaking. More so than romantic marriages."

"Because the arrangements are so well orchestrated by fathers like yours? Lovingly and with great concern for the participants? Or because neither party cares very much?"

"The latter, I'd think," she said, ignoring the sardonic way he'd asked that, though he could see by that gleam in her gaze that she'd heard it. "In our case, anyway. Once you've overcome your shock at finding the wrong sister at the altar, of course."

Her gaze then was as arid as her voice, and Chase couldn't understand why he cared. When he knew he shouldn't.

"I was surprised to learn the notorious Ariella Elliott

had a sister in the first place," he said, with some attempt to make his voice less rough. "Somehow, that never came up in all those discussions with your father. Or in any of the articles I've seen about your sister over the years. Though there was no attempt to hide you at any of the dinners we both attended."

He still stood by the window, watching her as if doing so would lead to some grand revelation, and countered that restless thing in him that *wanted* things he refused to acknowledge by shoving his hands in the pockets of his trousers. Quite as if he worried he'd otherwise have to fight to keep them from her.

Zara smiled. It was a slap of perfectly courteous ice and told him a number of things he didn't wish to know about her.

"I don't date musicians or actors. I don't attend the sorts of parties that the paparazzi cover, much less stagger out of them under the influence of unsavory substances at un-godly hours of the morning. I like books better than peo-ple. None of that makes for interesting gossip, I'm afraid."

He regarded her with what he wished was a dispassion-ate cool. "What would the gossips say about you, then? Interesting or otherwise?"

There was something vulnerable about her soft mouth then, a darker sheen to her golden eyes, but her chin edged high and she didn't drop her gaze from his.

"Is this a little bit of friendly, husbandly interest?" she asked. "Or are you merely gathering ammunition?"

She wasn't at all what he'd expected. That turned in him like heat. Like need.

"Everything is ammunition, Zara. But only if you're at war."

A ghost of a smile flirted with her mouth then, and was gone in the next instant. "And we, of course, are not at war."

"This is our wedding night, is it not?"

She studied him for a moment, and he wished that things were different. That he was, to start. That she was anyone other than who she was. An Elliott and his wife.

"I'm writing a master's thesis in English Literature," she said after a moment. "My field of study is Gothic novels in popular culture. It's my father's opinion that I'd be better served getting a degree in something that made for better cocktail party conversation. Everybody has an opinion about *Romeo and Juliet*, for example. Why not study that instead of stupid books only hysterical women read?"

Chase was sidetracked from his own dark thoughts. "Your father has an objection to advanced degrees? Surely most parents would be proud." His own, for example.

"Academia is the refuge of the ugly and boring," she said, obviously quoting her father, and remarkably cool about it. It spoke to a long familiarity with Amos's insulting opinions, and Chase found he didn't like the idea of that at all. "While he acknowledges that it is thus a perfectly appropriate place for the likes of me, the fact remains that I'm *his* daughter. I ought to be a better bargaining chip. The kind of frat boy investment bankers he'd like to throw my way, because of who their fathers are and how such connections could benefit him, have no patience for women who think that much."

Chase could only stare at her.

Zara smiled, and it was even icier than before. "I'm paraphrasing."

He shook his head. "You must know that you are none of those things."

He didn't know why he'd said that. This wasn't a therapy session, and he was the last person who should have been offering advice to anyone. Zara's eyes chilled.

"I love being patronized," she said. "I really do. But I find it goes down a whole lot smoother with food."

And the fact was, this was war, and Zara was ammunition. That Amos Elliott was horrible to his own child shouldn't have surprised Chase at all. It didn't.

He had to stop pretending he was any different. That he was some kind of hero who could save anyone from anything. He already knew better, didn't he? He already knew exactly what he was. *Murderer.*

But this was about the future, not the past.

Chase rang for their dinner. Then he beckoned his enemy's daughter to the small table, took his own seat across from her and began the war in earnest.

"What are you doing in here?"

Zara jumped at the sound of Chase's voice, whirling around so the bookshelf was at her back and the mad beating of her heart as it tried to fly from her chest might not knock her down to the floor. She didn't know how she didn't scream—and then she saw him.

He stood a few feet away, dressed in the jeans, bare feet and casually buttoned shirt she'd learned he preferred, the messiness of his dark hair the only hint that it was an hour of the night when most people were asleep. He should have looked rumpled, but this was Chase Whitaker, so he looked *lethal* instead.

And the way he looked at her made everything inside of her roll up into a knot and *pulse.* She couldn't have screamed if she'd wanted to. She was too busy trying her best not to purr—and the fact that it didn't make sense that she should have this kind of reaction to a man she'd resolved she'd merely tolerate didn't make that knotted, pulsing thing ease.

If anything, it made it that much worse.

"I couldn't sleep," Zara said.

Unnecessarily, as her presence in the house's spacious, book-jammed library this long after midnight made that abundantly clear on its own. But it was better than sur-rendering to her traitorous body and making like a cat.

A December storm howled around the old stone house tonight, rattling the windows and making the floorboards creak ominously. Zara might have decided to keep her overactive imagination in check while she had to stay in this place but there was no sleeping through all of that.

So she'd crawled out of the soft, warm bed, pulled on the long, lush wool sweater she used as a kind of bathrobe, and padded down through the dark house to the library, where the fire was always blazing and the storm at the French doors made her feel cozy instead of vulnerable.

Quite the opposite of how her husband made her feel.

He studied her in that hooded way of his that made her feel like prey. And much too unreasonably warm for a night this close to full winter in upstate New York. In a drafty old stone house that might or might not have been haunted, the way old stone houses often were. *In your imagination, not in reality*, she reminded herself sharply—though it was the kind of two o'clock in the morning that blurred those lines.

Zara swallowed hard as she moved away from the book-shelf, clutching the thick, eighteenth-century novel she'd selected to her chest as she made her way back to one of the deep, comfortable leather armchairs that sat before the fireplace. She curled herself up in it, her legs tucked up beneath her, and told herself she felt better no matter what racket her heart was making.

She wasn't surprised when Chase followed, settling himself across from her with that curious grace of his that she was certain could hypnotize her, if she let it. *Could and would.* And then he fixed her with that same, unwavering blue stare of his that made every hair on her body dance in instinctive response.

It had been a strange week.

"Welcome to your honeymoon," he'd said that first night in that little dining room where he insisted they take all their meals. He'd lounged there, pushing the shockingly good food around on his plate as if he was too restless to eat—*or too drunk*, she'd reminded herself sharply—and he'd watched her. He was always watching her. Looking for something she grew more and more sure she didn't want to name, especially not after she'd allowed him to see her naked. *Stop thinking about that*, she'd ordered herself. Fruitlessly. "It will last the month. We'll spend it here, in seclusion, as happily married new couples do."

"All the happily married new couples I know spend their entire honeymoons on this or that social media platform, tirelessly documenting every moment of their bliss," Zara had pointed out. "It's a sign of the times."

"It is not a sign of our times." His gaze had gone even darker, if possible. "You will contact whoever you must to let them know that you'll be out of touch for the remainder of December. Holidays included."

"You mean my thesis advisor?" She hadn't understood why she was responding to him as if he had the right to make declarations about how she'd spend her time, or where. Why she'd been pretending this was some kind of normal conversation when it was not. When the specter of her ill-conceived nudity had hung before them as if there had been another version of her lounging across the small table between them, as naked as she'd been in that bathtub. "There's no need. The semester is nearly over and I completed all my coursework last week."

She certainly hadn't understood why she'd told him *that*. Why not go traipse around in dark alleys, while she was at it? Why not write *victim* in big, bold letters on her forehead? She'd then reminded herself that as she was not, in fact, a Gothic heroine, there was no need to worry what she told this man.

"And aren't you lucky that I did," she'd continued then, her annoyance at herself bleeding through into her voice, "or I'd have to tell you exactly what you could do with all your orders. I'm not your subordinate, Chase. I'm your wife."

"Thank you." His voice had been cool. Sardonic. "I'm unlikely to forget that."

Zara had interpreted that as a slap. She'd told herself it was a good thing. Bracing and necessary. This man was much too tempting, and she didn't need or want to be sympathetic to him. She didn't need or want to *want* him, either. She only needed to survive this marriage long enough to make her point to her father, in so doing honoring her grandmother's last wish. *Sympathy* for the likes of Chase Whitaker was unnecessary.

Lust was suicidal.

"Since you asked," she'd said mildly, still holding that thrilling blue gaze of his, "I envision a marriage as a union of like-minded partners. In this case, we both seem to want the marriage to do something for us. How delightfully equal that makes us, don't you think?"

His mouth had twitched. "Is that what you call it?"

"I don't know what kind of arrangement you had with my sister," she'd said, her chin rising, because she hadn't wanted to know what agreements he and Ariella had come to—much less how they'd come to them. "But you should know that I don't do very well with overbearing asses who try to dictate my every move."

"Save your father."

"One overbearing ass in a girl's life is more than enough," she'd said, and had even laughed as if she'd found the whole thing frothy and fun, like an adventure—when she adamantly did not. "And the sad truth is that I have a tendency toward seething rebellion. I'm telling you up front, so there are no surprises down the line should you decide to go all…" She'd waved a hand at him, encompassing that brooding, ruthless thing that spiked the air all around him. "Grouchy."

And she'd have sworn on a stack of Bibles that was laughter in those wild blue eyes of his then, in that small curve of his intoxicating mouth.

"I don't believe anyone has ever called me *grouchy* in all my life."

Zara had smiled. "To your face."

He'd sat there, looking as much discomfited as he'd looked amused, for what had felt like a very long time.

"There is a company holiday party of sorts on New Year's Eve," he'd told her, long after she'd decided he wasn't going to speak again, that they'd simply sit in that pretty little room tucked away in that vast, echoing house until they'd turned to dust. "It's an annual affair, though I haven't attended very often in the past."

Zara had nodded slowly, trying to work out his angle and seeing nothing but those unsettling blue eyes and all the secrets they held.

"I've been to it many times," she'd said. And each time, her father had trotted Ariella out like she were the spoils of war while he'd either ignored Zara entirely or had made her feel like an interloper. *And this is my younger daughter*, he'd said one memorable year. *She's got a face for radio and spends most of her life with it in a book, anyway.* Charming. She'd preferred the years her invitation had been "accidentally overlooked." "I can't believe you ever had something more exciting to do than waft about the Whitaker Industries offices all night, waiting for the year to end. You've been missing out."

"I've no doubt." He'd finally moved his gaze from hers, but only to toy with that ever-present glass of amber liquid before him, and it hadn't helped. Zara had still felt *caught*.

Held tight, like he was the spider and this was all a great web. "It will be our first appearance as husband and wife."

"I'm sure the grateful masses will pay us an extraordinary tribute," she'd said drily. "Particularly after our month of seclusion, the better to whet their appetites. We might as well be your British royalty."

He'd raised his eyes to hers then, and it had amazed her, the force of them, the *punch* of all that blue, as if she hadn't seen them a scant moment before. She'd wondered if she'd ever get used to it. Or if it would always be like that when she was near him. If he would always stun her.

"This time, wear something that fits you," he'd said.

And she'd stopped thinking about his eyes.

Now she sat there before him in all that brooding silence broken only by the crackle and pop of the fire within and the rush of the storm without, and Zara couldn't take it. She didn't like where her mind went when she was around him. She felt far too many things she didn't want to feel. This had never been about him, after all. It had been something she'd let her father sweep her into because she'd thought it might solve things between them the way Grams had wanted. Or—because she was a realist, down there beneath the part of her that heard a creak in a floorboard and thought *ghost*—give her a better bargaining chip with him. Chase himself had been an afterthought.

Funny then, that she'd thought a great deal about Chase and not at all about her father since she'd arrived here a week ago.

"Have you rung your sister?" he asked now.

It sounded like such an idle question. But it was somewhere in the neighborhood of two-fifteen in the morning, and if Zara had learned anything from this week in Chase Whitaker's presence, it was that he was very rarely idle. About anything. No matter the role he seemed to play in all the gossip columns.

"At this hour?" she asked. Stalling.

The twitch of his mouth indicated he knew exactly what she was doing.

"If I'm remembering your sister's habits correctly, this would be an excellent time to reach her," he pointed out. "She's almost certainly awake and about."

"Exactly how well do you know Ariella?" Zara asked.

Something like amusement, though it was too hard to be only that, gleamed in his blue eyes then, and she realized a bit too late that she'd sounded much too sharp. Sharp the way one might sound if she cared, when Zara knew full well she shouldn't. *She didn't.*

She wouldn't let herself.

"That sounds a bit loaded, doesn't it?" On another man, that might have been a smile. On Chase, it only made everything seem perilous. "I'm not sure that's a question I should answer."

"You're very interested in whether or not I've spoken to her," Zara pointed out, in a far more reasonably moderate tone of voice. "You ask me every day."

"She did stand me up at an altar," Chase said in that same deceptively casual voice, though Zara had to restrain her urge to shudder at the intensity beneath it. "That does tend to focus the attention. Or, at the very least, require some kind of discussion after the fact."

He shifted in his chair, calling attention to that rangy, athletic body of his. He was simply too beautiful. His was a kind of savage elegance, evident despite the way he lounged there as if he was something other than ruthless. There wasn't a single thing about him she trusted.

But she couldn't seem to look away, either.

"I'm not one of Ariella's priorities," Zara said after a moment, ignoring that softly singing thing inside of her, the pitched heat that felt like a ruinous melody from deep beneath her skin. That awful longing she refused to acknowledge. "She hasn't called me."

He continued to study her for a long moment, then he shifted all of that brooding focus of his to the fire, leaving Zara feeling simultaneously released and bereft.

Ariella hadn't called. Zara hadn't lied.

But she hadn't seen fit to mention that Ariella had responded to Zara's texts and voice mails with a text of her own. In her own sweet time. She'd written the day before:

This is like a coup for you. You should enjoy it while you can. It's not like there's any other way you'd date someone like Chase, is there?

That was her explanation for disappearing on her own wedding morning. That was her apology for leaving Zara to clean up her mess, and it was her thanks, too.

That was the only response Zara had got.

It was so typical that Zara had screamed. Into one of her pillows, facedown on that fluffy bed that belonged to another woman too much like her sister, who would never have received a text like that from anyone, and who would never, therefore, have had to deal with all its nasty undercurrents.

She'd told herself that she didn't care. That Ariella's obnoxious insinuations were designed to hurt her, which was precisely why she shouldn't let them. She'd focused on her work instead, reading several of the books on critical theory she needed to incorporate into the current chapter of her thesis and working on her ever-expanding bibliography.

But it was very late on a very dark night now, Chase Whitaker was the most dangerously beautiful man Zara had ever been this close to and it was like Ariella was standing right behind her the way she'd done as a mean-spirited teenager, whispering her little poisons straight into Zara's ear.

The arranged marriage Zara had been forced to undertake in Ariella's stead was a *coup*, because Zara couldn't expect to marry anyone under her own devices. Much less someone like Chase, who was *obviously* miles out of Zara's league. Zara could hardly dream she'd ever *date* someone like him. Ariella thought she should *enjoy it* because, of course, this must be like a fantasy brought to life for sad, lonely, fat and ugly Zara.

It didn't matter whether Zara believed these things. She was a twenty-six-year-old woman, not a sixteen-year-old, and she knew better than to listen to her nasty family members and their tired old refrains about who she was in their eyes. What mattered was that Ariella had become so much like their father that she'd felt comfortable spewing that kind of thing at her only sister in a *text*. Like she really and truly believed she'd done Zara a *favor*.

Zara realized she was scowling the same moment she felt the weight of Chase's attention again.

"Why are you always barefoot?" she asked quickly, because she didn't want to give him the opportunity to yank the truth from her. She hadn't liked how it had felt when she'd told him her father's feelings about her master's degree. It was one thing to experience her own family in all their dysfunctional glory. It was worse, somehow, to share it. Especially with a man like him. It was impossible to imagine him putting up with the same kind of nonsense. From anyone. "Have you lost all feeling in your feet? It's cold outside and this house is made primarily of old, drafty stone."

Again, that little crook in his lips that was his version of a smile that Zara found she liked—and looked forward to coaxing out of him—a great deal more than she should. Like it was their own personal version of happiness. Contentment. Newly wedded bliss.

You need to get a grip on yourself, Zara, she told herself then. *Right now. You'd be better off chasing ghosts down the hallways, and far more successful at that.*

"I've spent most of my life in England," Chase said. He sounded conversational—which was so unlike him that Zara viewed it as a personal victory. "It's cold here, but dry. It doesn't get in the bones in quite the same way."

"Didn't you grow up here?" she asked, startled. "I thought I was staying in your sister's childhood bedroom."

She couldn't define the expression she saw on his face then. As guarded as it was intent, that hint of any kind of easiness gone as if it had never been. She was certain he wouldn't answer her—and couldn't entirely hide her surprise when he did.

"This was my father's house," he said, sounding very careful, as if he was making his way across eggshells and glass, and Zara wished she could see them. Or help, somehow. "It was handed down from his grandfather, who built it to compete with the likes of the Rockefellers and all the other grand houses up and down the Hudson River. My parents used this as their primary residence, but I spent the bulk of my time in school in England. Mattie was here far more than I ever was. Especially after our mother died."

"I read about that." She'd scoured the internet, in fact, for every tidbit ever written about any member of the Whitaker family. She told herself she couldn't help it, that she was a researcher at heart, as her master's degree course proved. That she had no personal stake in any of it, that she felt *absolutely nothing* when she read this *Vanity Fair* article about his late mother, Lady Daphne, or that tabloid paean to his overly observed love life. Nothing at all. "I'm sorry."

She thought there was something hollow in his gaze then, something so broken it made her hurt, but told herself it had to be the shadows all around them. The hour. Those terrible songs that moved in her that made her despair of herself.

When he spoke again his voice was almost too low. "It was a long time ago."

"My mother isn't dead," she said. She didn't know why. "But she was never quite right after my father divorced her. Grief can take any number of forms, I mean. Even extraordinary selfishness."

He studied her, and Zara didn't know why she felt so *stricken* suddenly. As if everything had shifted all around them and gone somehow wrong.

"They say time cures everything," he said after a moment, but she knew—*she knew*—that he wasn't the least bit cured. That time did nothing for him but pass.

Around them, the library was a vast, high room, but tonight it felt small. Close. Like it was only the two of them in a cave somewhere, warding off the storm. It felt much too intimate.

And that was the last thing she wanted with this man, because Zara knew herself. She didn't do casual. She didn't *enjoy herself* in any of the ways Ariella had meant she should. She couldn't. She wasn't built that way—and this marriage wasn't built to last out the season.

But he isn't casual at all, a voice inside of her whispered. *He's your* husband, *no matter how you got to the altar. He is the very definition of* not *casual.*

It was amazing how tempting it was to listen.

But Zara knew better.

"I think it's time I tried to get some sleep," she said, her voice little more than a whisper. A small scrape against the warmth, the closeness, that look in his eyes and the things that surged in her like an answer she didn't want to hear.

Like that same song deep inside of her, changing her with every note.

His mouth crooked, and he watched her like he could see all of her confusion right there on her face.

Like it was a challenge. A gauntlet on the floor at her feet.

"Good night, Chase," she whispered, and then she fled.

CHAPTER FOUR

SHE WAS DRIVING him crazy.

Chase let her race from the room, glancing at the grand-father clock on the far wall and noting it was nearly time for his end of the workday call to Tokyo. He knew Zara thought he rattled around this house all night in some kind of drunken stupor. He encouraged it.

Just as he'd encouraged the British press to portray him as a pretty boy of no depth whatsoever, happy to whore himself around Europe and play at a corporate job in Dad-dy's company as it suited him. The great part about having discovered his own dark depths at thirteen, he knew, was that he'd stopped caring very much about any bad reputa-tion he might have thereafter.

So there was no reason at all it should have bothered him that Zara Elliott looked at him like he might well be the very monster he knew he was. That she was the first one who'd ever looked at him as if she *knew*, as if she could see straight through twenty years of pretense to the truth.

What he didn't understand was why he wanted her all the more because of it.

"You are a twisted, terrible man," he muttered, glaring at the fire. But he already knew that.

He might have declared this a honeymoon, but that was mostly so he'd have some breathing room to prepare the counterattack that would rid him of his Amos Elliott problem at last. His merger with his new brother-in-law's company was moving forward as planned. Nicodemus and he had come to a number of agreements on key issues, which meant everything was falling into place, exactly as he'd planned in the desperate days when he'd realized he and his sister had no choice but to go ahead with these medieval arranged marriages. That it was the only thing that could save the company, and thus the two of them, too. Or their father's legacy, anyway.

Revenge was going to be more than sweet, Chase thought then. He knew he couldn't change the past. He couldn't undo what he'd done. He couldn't bring back his mother or be the son his father had deserved. But he could save Whitaker Industries. He could preserve the second great love of his father's life. And he could cut Amos Elliott down to size while he did it.

Zara was the key. But she wasn't behaving the way he'd thought she would. Correction: the way he'd thought her sister would.

He'd understood everything there was to know about Ariella Elliott within three seconds of meeting her. She'd shimmied about before him, all jaded eyes and come-hither lips, and he'd been as bored as if he'd actually dated her for months. It was one of the reasons he'd agreed to Amos's insane demands so easily. He knew her type. He'd met thousands of Ariellas in his day. Apathetic. Entitled. Awash in a sea of her own self-importance and buoyed in her narcissism by all her father's money and influence. He couldn't think of a single thing a woman like Ariella could do that would surprise him.

A long December locked up in this house with Ariella would already have gone differently. That first night in that bathroom would have ended in an entirely more physical manner, Chase was well aware. By now he could have moved on to other things, like the troweled-on compli-

ments and feigned interest that would lead a woman like
Ariella to talk. To talk and talk and talk, indiscreet and
self-satisfied, secure in her misguided belief that any man
she condescended to sleep with remained forever under
her spell.

It would have been easy.

But Zara was nothing like her sister.

This Elliott sister required thought, and the more Chase
tried to puzzle her out, the more he found himself remembering her standing in that bath, slick and warm and so
stunning it still raced through him, hot and wild. And he
had the very disconcerting notion that just like that night,
if he touched her, he wouldn't be in control at all.

Not to mention his very real concern that if he tried to
use her for information the way he'd planned to do with her
sister, she'd know exactly what he was doing. He couldn't
decide if he found that irritating or, much worse, arousing.

He heard her footsteps on the floor above him, moving down that long hall to her rooms, no doubt to lock
herself away from him the way she should. He heard the
storm outside the library windows, hurling itself against
the side of the house like it wanted to fight its way in. His
usual ghosts took up their positions around him, almost
like old friends after all this time. His mother on that last
day, laughing the way she'd always done, with her whole
body and such easy, captivating delight. His sister the way
she'd been back then, young and bright and happy, her little
girl's voice singing a song he'd spent a lifetime trying to
forget. His father when he'd still laughed so large, so un-
fettered, like he had nothing at all to lose, before the day
that Chase had proved him wrong forever.

The worst thing about Zara was that she made him remember, if only for moments here and there, what it had
felt like to be happy.

Unforgivable, he thought harshly.

Because this time, Chase knew exactly what he'd have to do to her, no matter that she was nothing like that terrible sister of hers who he wouldn't have minded using as a simple, effective tool to get what he wanted. This time, he knew what it would cost her when he did the thing he needed to do.

And the price he'd have to pay when he did it anyway.

Chase might have been the perfect Gothic hero, all brooding and dark and occasionally windswept as if to add to his mystique, but Zara spent a lot of her energy during the daylight hours making certain that the rest of this new married life was nothing like the books she studied. The house had a name, it was true, but no one invoked it in ponderous tones or acted like the house itself was alive and/or angry at its occupants.

"It's called Greenleigh," Mrs. Calloway, the housekeeper, had told her when she'd asked. "Just wait until spring and you'll see why. It's so pretty, with the lawns and the trees stretching out halfway to Poughkeepsie. The original Mr. Whitaker's wife's name was Leigh, so he named the place after her as a gift."

Zara was thrilled to discover that Mrs. Calloway was neither dour nor disapproving. She didn't waft through the house in shades of black, muttering alarming things about the past. Instead, she was a friendly older woman who bustled rather than walked, insisted upon decking the halls in as much Christmas cheer as it was possible to cram into one house and cooked like a dream. Her husband— who sang Christmas carols as he puttered about, in a surprisingly lovely tenor—had never been in Zara's presence without also being wreathed in smiles. They lived out in one of the guest cottages that dotted the estate and were more than happy to talk about their cheerful, well-adjusted children and their growing tally of plump grandchildren.

Despite first appearances and the slightest bit of hysteria brought on by impersonating Ariella, she group texted her three best friends from college, who lived all over the place these days and had been universally unimpressed to hear about her sudden wedding on the news, my actual marriage appears to be anything but supernatural.

A conviction that was not shared by the general public, insofar as the tabloids could be held to represent their views.

Society Shocker! they'd screamed that first week, right after the wedding. *Hottie Chase Spurns Ariella for Ugly Duckling Sis!*

And that was one of the more flattering headlines. When one week became two and neither Chase nor Zara appeared in public, they'd dropped any pretense of "flattery."

Ariella could have written those headlines herself, her friend Amy texted back staunchly from Denver after Zara shared the worst of them. They're as nasty as she is.

I suggest you ignore them, Marilee had chimed in from Chicago, and concentrate on that hot husband of yours.

I know I am, Isobel texted from Edinburgh.

Zara laughed out loud in her little sitting area before the fire, which had fast become her favorite part of her bedroom suite.

Relax, ladies, she texted back. It's not real.

But what worried her was how much she wanted it to be real. How much she wished and yearned and longed, like the sad little ugly duckling her sister and the whole world imagined she was already.

It was maddening. It was like being thirteen years old all over again, ungainly and insecure.

"Did I offend you in some way?" Chase asked at their usual dinner that night, cooped up in that tiny little room that seemed smaller all the time.

That was when Zara realized she was scowling at him. She forced herself to stop, to cast around for that polite smile she'd worn so easily before she'd met him. For years.

"Not recently," she said. "But I'm sure we need only wait a few moments before you remedy that."

And there was that little crook to those perfect lips of his that she spent more time fantasizing about than she should. Because she remembered all too well how they'd felt against hers in that church. The press of heat. The whisper of power in it. The way it had ricocheted through her body and lodged low in her belly, like a punch.

"No doubt," he agreed. "Mrs. Calloway tells me you were interrogating her about my ancestors again today. You need only ask me what you want to know, Zara. I'm a walking encyclopedia of all things Whitaker."

Zara had run into the housekeeper in one of the salons, dusting the forbidding portraits of old, steely-eyed men hanging there. Zara had grown up with a number of similar paintings in her father's rambling old house in Connecticut, many of them involving those silly Revolutionary War–era wigs she still couldn't take seriously.

"I very much doubt that the word *interrogate* was used," she said now. *So we both grew up surrounded by pompous portraits*, she told herself derisively. *That doesn't mean a thing. They aren't a bridge between you— they're paintings.* She really was pathetic, she thought, and sniffed. "And I'm not all that interested in your ancestors. I have far too many of my own. Also, I read your Wikipedia page."

He leaned back in his chair, looking as if he was actually enjoying himself, and Zara felt a warm sort of glow spill through her. Like that had been her goal all along.

Wasn't it? that traitorous little voice asked.

Chase was wearing a sweater tonight, a sleek, dark knit that was obviously soft as it pulled against the width of

those shoulders of his and drew attention to the easy perfection of his physique. But he was more than simply *hot*.
He exuded something raw and primal, something that kept
her belly in a tight knot whenever she was with him. Something that made her breasts heavy and her core slick, and
she'd never felt anything like it before.

She was an imperfect Gothic heroine, Zara knew. She
wasn't chaste or virginal. She'd always thought she was
as reasonably experienced as anyone her age, after the
boyfriend she'd had for the last two years of college and
the other one she'd had for about eighteen months before
graduate school. Not too much, not too little. She'd thought
she'd known what it was to want, to need, to *lust*, but she'd
never met anyone like Chase before.

This—*he*—was something new.

It was like everything had been the same before she'd
met him. Primary colors, bleeding one into the next, indistinguishable from each other. But Chase was rich, deep
blacks contrasted by stark whites. Arresting. Incandescent.
Moody. He was something deeper than what she'd known.
Something *more*.

And it occurred to her that her friends—and even Ariella and all the mean-spirited tabloids—were right. This
was an opportunity, and not one that came along very
often. How often did a scholar of Gothic novels get the
opportunity to spend this kind of time with her very own
Gothic hero?

Zara knew she wasn't hideous. She'd come to terms
with the differences between herself and the Ariellas of
the world a long time ago—it had been that or simply succumb to how wretched that gap made her feel. But even so,
Chase Whitaker was not the sort of man she'd ever have
imagined she'd find herself with, under any circumstances.
She preferred men who were more like her. Quirky. Brainy.
More *interesting* than *incandescent*.

Capable of fading into the background instead of commanding the attention of the whole room by the simple virtue of entering it.

Chase was wild blue, uncontainable, and she was stuck with him for at least the rest of the month of December. After that party on New Year's Eve that was obviously important to him for reasons she doubted he'd share with her, she imagined they'd wash their hands of each other. *You'll have your life back*, she told herself fiercely to cover that odd little hollow feeling at the thought.

And in the meantime, she didn't trust him or his motives for this marriage or his seeming obedience to her father's wishes—but why did she have to? She didn't want *trust*. She didn't want to *date* him.

She just *wanted*.

It didn't matter if she couldn't do casual under normal circumstances. What was *normal* here? This marriage had an expiration date on it already. Casual or serious or neither—it would take care of itself.

"Careful," Chase said then, and Zara realized she'd been staring at his mouth. "I might get the wrong idea."

She put her knife and fork down on her plate carefully. Very carefully. She lifted her gaze to all that raw blue. She breathed in, then out, and told herself there wasn't any part of her that might regret this rash decision.

You might as well enjoy yourself after all, that little voice whispered deep inside her, *and not only because Ariella is absolutely certain you won't.*

She hadn't asked to be in this situation. She'd been pushed. Dragged up the aisle, in fact. Why not indulge herself? Why not view this strange marriage of hers as *research*—and why not get the most out of her primary source while she could?

Zara smiled at him. Her husband, at least for now. And the most beautiful creature she'd ever beheld.

"But what if I want you to get the wrong idea?" she asked as casually as if she was discussing the weather.

"I'm sorry?"

She let her smile widen. "Just because this isn't a traditional marriage, it doesn't mean we're obligated to overlook all the benefits of one. We can pick and choose, surely."

"Let me make certain I understand you." She couldn't describe that look in his eyes then. More than wild. Deeper than primitive. So hot she lost herself for a moment. So bold she wasn't sure she'd ever breathe again. "You're not talking about sharing my surname, I assume. Or the dispensation of property."

There was a time she might have hesitated. Gone for the indirect approach to suss out his interest before committing herself. Before *revealing* herself. And it wasn't as if Chase was remotely *safe*, which had been the only reason she'd ever risked such things in the past.

She had no idea what came over her, but she decided she liked it. Her last recklessly spontaneous act had been to show him her naked body. How could propositioning him be any worse?

"I'm talking about consummation, that most traditional of marital acts," Zara said very deliberately, and watched him go still.

Very, very still.

She leaned forward so that her elbows were on the table and she could keep her gaze steady on his. Even if the blue of it burned and the deep fire there made her whole body feel shivery and *alive* again. Alive at last, no matter how reckless this was. No matter if she'd live to regret it.

At least she'd live.

"I'm talking about sex, Chase," she clarified. "With you."

Zara didn't regret it the moment she said it—but she certainly felt it drop through her like a stone. Hard and swift. Impossible to take back.

She told herself she didn't want to.

"Say that again," Chase ordered her, his voice low and rough.

He still didn't move. But then, he didn't laugh, either. If anything, he looked...*electric*. She could see he hadn't even twitched, so it made no sense that he seemed bigger somehow. As if all of those things she'd sensed in him— that brooding power, that sheer, masculine *force*—were unleashed now, and crowded out the air in the room.

He was immense. Wild. And she'd never wanted anyone more.

Zara considered him for a moment while her heart executed some kind of frantic ballet inside her chest, and she was certain the heat she could feel sizzling between them and making it difficult to breathe was splashed across her face. Like a beacon.

She was as subtle as a searchlight and she wasn't sure she cared.

"Which part?" she asked, because she enjoyed the tussle. The clash and roll of wits.

And because she was stalling. Still.

"Come here," he growled at her.

She felt it everywhere, like a touch. Like that low, commanding voice of his was wired directly to all of her secret places, to all of that desperate hunger she'd felt since the moment they'd locked eyes in that church. And everywhere she felt the caress of it, so rough and so raw, she felt a heavy kind of ache.

Need.

"I don't take orders," she said instead of obeying him, spurred on by some demon thing inside of her she didn't understand.

His mouth curved, and it was a hard, compelling thing. A stamp of sheer maleness, sex and desire, and she had to let out a hard breath to absorb it without dissolving where she sat.

"You will." He sounded certain.

"Are you sure you're interested?" she asked, instead of doing what that melting thing inside her wanted her to do, which was hurl herself at him in total abandon. And then do whatever he asked her to do, again and again and— "I ask because I did stand in front of you completely naked and your response was to tell me I'd best be on time for dinner."

The curve of his mouth became a smile, the first real one she'd seen on him, and it was devastating. It should have been impossible, but he became even more beautiful. Even more powerfully *him*. The smile made a celebration of that perfect face of his, those wicked brows, that mouth. It made his eyes gleam a brighter shade of blue, the blue of whole, perfect summers, all there in that single smile.

It made him irresistible, and Zara was certain he knew it.

"I haven't forgotten," he assured her, and he shifted in his seat then, lounging there as if he was relaxed when she could see that he wasn't. That he was in the grip of the same tension that held her.

But now that she'd brought up that night in the bath, and all the demons and specters she'd summoned along with it, she couldn't let it go.

"I'm not my sister," she said, her voice tighter than it should have been.

His gaze slammed into her. "A fact, Zara, of which I am well aware."

"And I don't want anything like pity sex, thanks," she continued, and though the words left claw marks on their way out, she managed to say it in a brash sort of way. As if it didn't hurt.

"Pity sex?" He looked thunderstruck.

"No substitutions," she said expansively, smiling as if she was calm, though she could feel the heat on her cheeks that proved she was a liar. "No closing your eyes in the dark and pretending it's the other Elliott sister beneath you." She couldn't believe she'd said that, and from the way his eyes widened, neither could he. "Or on top," she continued, as if *more talking* would make it any better. "I mean, no need to consign anyone to any traditional gender—"

"Zara."

Thank God he'd interrupted. She felt so out of control it was like a kind of dizziness, except she wasn't at all worried she'd get sick. She was more worried she'd keep talking herself into complications and then what?

"Shut up," he said in that sexy growl of his, and she did.

He studied her, the way he always did, except this time it left a trail of fire and hunger everywhere his blue gaze lit.

"Come here," he said again, and it was a dark, starkly sexual command. It shivered over her like a touch. Like that press of his lips against hers on that altar. Like he wanted her this hungry. This lit up and on fire. His mouth crooked up again, and that was the only reason she didn't simply burst, she thought. "Quietly."

Then he settled back in his chair and waited.

And Zara understood that this was not the first time Chase Whitaker had made these demands of a woman. She had no doubt that he knew exactly what he was doing, that he'd tested out this sort of thing a hundred times before. On some level, she supposed she should have been horrified by that. Unnerved, certainly, by someone whose experience so vastly outstripped hers. Alarmed by the sheer *certainty* in the way he waited, with all of that brash male confidence, for her to do as he bid her.

She was sure she should have felt *something* other than that dark, glimmering thread that wound inside of her, tighter by the second, miraculous and real.

"What will I do when I get there?" she asked. Mostly to disobey his order that she be quiet.

He smiled again, and it was a dark, thrilling thing. It connected to that knot deep inside of her and pulsed. Long and low and hard.

"I'm certain you'll think of something, clever girl that you are," he murmured.

And she knew that most girls, clever or not, would stand and walk around the table. They'd take the opportunity to roll their hips, pout a little bit, give the man a show. Or anyway, girls like her sister would do that, because they always did. Zara had *seen* Ariella do it to this or that boyfriend over the years. And she considered it. She had a brilliant flash of herself standing before him, then sinking down to her knees between those long legs of his...

But Zara didn't want to be *most girls*. She didn't want to compete. She didn't want to be anything like Ariella.

Ever.

Once again, Zara didn't think. She leaned forward and pushed all their plates to the side. Then, without giving herself time to second-guess it, she pulled herself up and onto the strong oak table that she'd admired for its lovely polish as well as its sturdiness over the past two weeks and launched herself across it.

Her reward was the way he almost came out of his chair, then caught himself. The way his blue eyes went supernova and every one of those long, athletic lines of his body went taut.

"What the bloody hell are you doing?"

But he said it like he couldn't believe it was really happening, not like it horrified him.

And Zara laughed. Like launching herself to her feet in the bath that night, she hadn't thought this through. Unlike then, this felt good. It was good to move. To slide her hands out over the smooth wood in front of her, reveling in the tactile pleasure of it, like it was that ridged wonder he called his abdomen. To let her hair fall all around her like she was as wild as he was, yet sensual and distinctly feminine. To push forward, her knees on the table, all of her in motion, answering that howling thing inside of her. To *do something* with all that crackling electricity inside of her that she thought might incinerate her otherwise.

"I have no idea," she replied, and she hardly recognized her own voice. Thick and needy and powerful, somehow, all the same.

And then she was right there, her face before his. And he wasn't lounging in his chair anymore, like some dissolute playboy king. His face had gone hard and almost feral, his eyes glittering with need and that mouth of his a hard, gloriously male line.

She trembled deep inside.

And Chase didn't ask her any more questions.

He reached over and speared his fingers directly into the mess of her hair, his palms at her cheekbones.

She made a sound of need. Of sheer, unadulterated greed.

He laughed then, and it was a triumphant sound. Dark and profoundly masculine, and it rolled through her, hot and dry, and only fanned the flames higher. And then he dragged her mouth to his.

This was no press of lips like that silly ritual he'd adhered to in the church. This had nothing to do with her damned father. This was a reckoning. This was long overdue.

This was more necessary than breath.

It was a taking.

He ravaged her mouth. He took and he tasted, and Zara met him. Every stroke. Every angle of his jaw. Every thrust of his tongue. She lost herself in the exquisite perfection of his taste. Rough. Male. And the hint of whiskey.

She wanted to drown in him.

That wild electricity danced between them, slick and

mad. She couldn't find the right angle. He couldn't seem to get close enough.

Zara wanted him with an intensity that might have alarmed her, had she cared about anything but the sheer exultation of his mouth moving against hers. That heart-stopping taste, like something she'd once known well and had lost.

Like recognition, she thought.

Like home.

And she understood that she was never going to survive this man. But his hands tightened in her hair, he held her jaw where he wanted it and he plundered her mouth with as much consummate skill as greed, and Zara couldn't bring herself to do anything but kiss him back.

Again and again and again.

CHAPTER FIVE

MINE.

The word pounded through him with every deep, drugging taste of her. Like a drumbeat. Louder than his own heart.

Like this would never be enough. Like it had nothing to do with revenge.

Chase tore his mouth from hers, shoved his chair back from the damned table and then hauled her the rest of the way across it until she tumbled over his lap and he could arrange her there the way he wanted her.

Or one of the ways he wanted her.

"Better," he muttered when he'd settled her with her legs over his and her arms around his neck. Not astride him, not yet, or he thought he might explode like a teenager.

And then he claimed her mouth once more.

It was more than *better.* That lush bottom he'd lusted after in the bath was nestled up against the hardest part of him, urging him on. Making him feel more animal than man. Every time she shivered, he felt it like a stroke of her hand.

And the deeper he kissed her, the more she met him, the wilder it got. And the more she shivered.

Mine, he thought again, a primitive hunger that should have alarmed him surging through him. *My wife.*

He kept one hand tangled in that gorgeous fall of her

hair, that riot of reds, and let the other one explore the body that had haunted him night and day throughout this cursed week. All of those breathtaking curves, right there beneath his palm. All of that stunning lushness *right here* in his arms. At last.

He traced his way down the sensual line of her back, that he could *see* as if she still stood naked before him. She was wearing a clingy shirt made of a soft, sleek fabric that moved with her and made her curves that much more enticing.

He thought she might kill him. He wasn't sure he'd mind.

Chase wrenched his mouth from hers and followed the line of her neck down toward that soft shoulder visible in the wide neckline of her shirt, licking his way across the lightly scented expanse of her skin.

Zara sighed. It was a broken, needy sound, and he felt it in his sex. Like she'd leaned over and taken him deep in her mouth.

He thought he'd never been this drunk in his life. Completely and utterly intoxicated by this woman, so rocked he couldn't tell if he'd ever feel sober again. And he didn't think he cared.

"Chase," she said, and it took him longer than it should have to realize that was his name. That it was not only his name, but that she wanted him to stop what he was doing and listen. Or worse, *talk*.

"Quiet," he told her, and he thought he sounded fierce, but she laughed. "I'm busy."

"I can see that," she said, her voice shaking with laughter and lust, and something bright shot through him. Like a bolt of sunlight, and he didn't want to know what that meant. He didn't want to dig into it. He used his teeth against the gentle rounding that was her collarbone instead, and felt that quiver all the way through her.

"I don't know what you're used to here in these wild, uncivilized colonies," he continued, moving back up her neck, tasting her as he went, collecting those shivers of hers like pieces of gold he could hoard, "but I take my traditional duties rather seriously. I can assure you that I attend to them with diligence—" and he found the curve of her earlobe then, taking it between his teeth in a little scrape that made her breath catch "—and focus."

On that he shifted, dropping one hand to hold her hip and the other moving to cradle her face in his palm. Too-bright gold in her eyes and that carnal mouth of hers. His undoing.

"But—"

He didn't want to hear whatever she was about to say. He licked his way into her mouth instead, like she was his dessert. And she melted against him, like she thought so, too.

And then he simply kissed her.

Until he forgot why he'd ever thought he shouldn't. Until there was nothing in the whole world but the taste of her mouth, her hair all around them like a sweet curtain and the way she moved against him as she sat there draped over his lap.

Until he didn't know which of them was which.

She pulled her mouth from his, and Chase didn't know if minutes had passed, or years. Lifetimes. When he failed to care about that, too, an alarm went off in some dim, dark recess inside him, but he ignored it.

"Stop," she whispered when he moved as if to claim her mouth again. "Listen."

He stopped. It took a moment for that greedy hunger to loosen its hold on him. For that roar inside him—lust and need and that pounding thing that was his heart—to ease back enough that he was less primitive, more man again.

So close to that monster in him, he thought darkly. Capable of anything, even here.

That was so unpalatable that it took him another moment to realize he could hear someone outside in the hallway. Mrs. Calloway, no doubt, right on time to clear their plates and serve their actual dessert.

"I heard the door close," Zara told him, her golden eyes huge and her voice still a whisper. "I think she walked in first."

Reality was like a roundhouse kick to the face.

Chase gathered Zara up and set her on her feet, then stood, furious. Blackly, consumingly furious. At himself.

What the hell was he doing? How had he forgotten himself entirely—again? What had happened to his self-control—necessary for the plotting required here? But of course, he knew. It was Zara. That teasing lilt in her voice. That challenging glint in her eyes. That damned body of hers he thought might be the end of him in all those lush, gorgeous curves.

He stalked to the door and wrenched it open, nodding stiffly at Mrs. Calloway by way of bidding her enter. Then he had to stand there and suffer through the storm battering at him, in all its rage and blackness and the bleak things beneath, as she swept in the way she always did, chattering and smiling.

"Should have known better than to burst in unannounced on a pair of newlyweds," she practically sang. "Can't apologize enough!"

Chase's gaze slid to the brand-new wife he would not have referred to as a newlywed, given all those implications, and he simply froze.

Because she was smiling back at Mrs. Calloway, standing right where he'd put her as if she'd forgotten how to move. Her face was bright red with embarrassment and leftover passion. Her hair was a tousled mess that showed him—and, no doubt, Mrs. Calloway—exactly what his hands had been doing moments before. She'd crossed her arms beneath her breasts, and he doubted she realized how that emphasized them, how that drew his attention directly to those pretty nipples so obviously tight and hard beneath her shirt. Her mouth was faintly swollen from his, and she was *smiling* as if all of this was precisely what it looked like.

As if they were simple, run-of-the-mill, everyday newlyweds who couldn't keep their hands off each other. Nothing more, nothing less.

And it pierced him as surely as if she'd hurled a spear at him, as if it had bored a hole straight through him, how much he wanted it to be true in that moment. He could *see* it. What it would be like if they were those people. If, when the door closed, they would laugh and start all over again, basking in their shared closeness. Their happiness.

Whatever it was that people felt when they were crazy in love with each other and not in the least bit afraid to show it.

Chase had never felt it himself, nor anything close. He'd always dated forgettable women, interchangeable women. He knew they'd bore him before they went out on their first date, so he'd always chosen them for other reasons. How their presence on his arm might benefit him. Whether or not they photographed well. Some or other lust, though nothing like what had swamped him tonight. What still beat in him now, heavy and low, testing his control.

He knew what it looked like, though. That kind of love. He'd seen it a very long time ago in his own parents. They'd sparkled when they'd been together, as if they'd been plugged in to their very own electric current. They'd held hands. They'd each smiled bright and happy when the other had walked into the room. They'd glowed.

And then you killed all that, the cold judge who presided over the darkest part of him pronounced. Lest he forget who he was. Or what he'd done. *You killed her. And them.*

"Now I understand why you married so quickly!" Mrs. Calloway said directly to him as she headed back for the door, snapping him back into the moment with her knowing little chuckle. "Enjoy this, Mr. Chase. You deserve it."

She might as well have elbowed him in the face, this kindly old woman whom he'd known the whole of his life and whom he knew wished him only good. It was that much of a body blow.

Because Chase knew exactly what he deserved. And it certainly wasn't whatever romantic fantasy his housekeeper had cooked up in her head. Not to mention what he'd been spinning out in his own.

And then Mrs. Calloway was gone, shutting the door very pointedly behind her as she sang back over her shoulder that there was no need to worry, they wouldn't be disturbed again. Not tonight.

"How embarrassing," Zara said as the other woman's footsteps sounded on the hall floor, then faded away, in that same voice she'd used before, that he'd determined was her nerves in action. He shouldn't find it adorable, he was well aware, and the fact that he did made him hate himself that much more. "I don't think I've ever been walked in on in my life. I can't decide if I'm humiliated or oddly—"

"I'm glad she walked in." Chase cut her off. He didn't miss the way she stiffened, or the coolness that crept into that gold gaze of hers. He told himself he didn't care about that. Because God knew, he shouldn't have. "That was a mistake."

Zara studied him then, and Chase felt…outsized. As if his skin no longer fit the way it had before. As if he'd lost complete control of himself and all those terrible things in him had burst free, distorting him where he stood.

As if she really could see all of that darkness in him for what it was.

"I'm sorry you think so," she said after a moment, and he didn't care that he knew her better now than to believe that calm tone she used. That he could see a far darker truth in the gaze she dropped from his an instant later.

And if I can see that after two weeks and a kiss, he thought, *what can she see in me?*

Chase felt his hands tightening into fists and ordered himself to breathe. To open them again. To claw back some goddamned control. He wasn't thirteen anymore. He was twenty years older than he'd been then, and these days, he knew how to handle himself.

Or he had before Zara Elliott had catapulted up that damned church aisle and into his life, dressed like a gazebo and capable of destroying his composure with a single look.

He hadn't expected this, he thought then, as this wife he hadn't wanted frowned at the floor like that might bring her clarity. He hadn't expected *her*. This all would have been different if he'd been dealing with her sister, who was so unmemorable he couldn't summon her features in his own head. If this had been Ariella, he wouldn't have been set on fire like this, even now, like there was a blaze in him that nothing could dim. Like all she need do was reach for him and he'd forget himself all over again.

Chase hadn't responded to a woman like this in as long as he could remember—perhaps ever—and that awful little fact all but flattened him. It also opened his eyes, at last, to the danger he was in. He had to remember his endgame here.

She was Amos Elliott's daughter, and that meant he needed to *use* her. Not *succumb* to her.

"Let's be honest for a moment," he said, not bothering to sound polite.

Zara laughed, a rueful little scrape of sound that Chase knew would haunt him later. He could add it to his expansive collection of ghosts and regrets.

"That's not an opening sentence that ever leads anywhere good," she pointed out. "Much like, 'I want to talk' or 'no offense, but...' Nothing anyone wants to hear ever follows."

She smiled in a hesitant sort of way, as if encouraging him to do the same, but Chase refused to be amused by her. *He refused.*

"This isn't going to last," he said shortly. Almost aggressively, and he saw that register in the way her body went tight. Too tight. Her arms, still crossed over her middle, stiffened like she was hugging herself. "This marriage is a joke. At best, a convenient vehicle. I need to be certain that when its usefulness has passed, there won't be any lingering confusion."

"Lingering confusion?" she repeated. Her head tilted and her gleaming eyes narrowed. "You mean mine, I'm guessing?"

What absurd thing had she said before? *Pity sex?* Chase could use that.

"You will fall in love." He shrugged when her glare glazed over into something far more hostile. "It's inevitable."

"And why is that?" Her tone was sharp.

"Please," he said dismissively, and with enough condescension that she stiffened further with obvious outrage. "The truth is, I don't want the mess. It's not worth the bother for something as easily obtained and equally forgettable as sex." He waited until he saw her temper bloom in bright red splashes across her cheeks, then went for the kill shot. "I can get that anywhere, Zara. You must know that. Your sister offered me a blow job within five minutes of our introduction."

She paled, then splashed scarlet again. But she didn't

keel over, this wife of his he wished he didn't want the way he did, like a searing fire in his blood. He supposed that would haunt him, too.

"Anyone can get sex anywhere, Chase," she retorted softly, his name a slap. "And a blow job is Ariella's version of a friendly handshake. I'm sorry if you thought it was something special, just for you."

So he sighed, and raked his hands through his hair and made a show of not quite rolling his eyes.

"You can't imagine you're the first woman to throw herself at me, can you?" he asked, his voice somewhere between patronizing and the sort of beleaguered kindness that he knew would appall her, it was so much like pity. "You're simply the first I've happened to be married to at the time. And I appreciate the thought, Zara. I do."

Her face was even redder then, and her eyes were so dark he could hardly see their color. But she stood there before him, drawn up to her full height, and he had the impression she was utterly impenetrable then. Like she'd wrapped herself in steel.

It was impossible not to admire her. He didn't fight it.

"You're the most beautiful man I've ever seen," she said, and her tone made the skin at the back of his neck tickle, because it was anything but complimentary. "But you're empty inside, aren't you? A shell of a thing, dressed up in pretty clothes and those lonely eyes, but really no more than a ghost walking around in the daytime. Like this house. An obsessively well-maintained mausoleum."

"Or possibly," he drawled out, his voice flat because he didn't want to admit the accuracy of the hit she'd just leveled at him or investigate the damage it had left behind, "I'm simply not interested."

She laughed at him then, and even though he could hear the hurt in it, he couldn't see it on her face. She'd locked him out and he hated it.

But he had no choice. If he couldn't control her—or more to the point, himself, when he touched her—he'd have to keep her at arm's length and find a different way to get his revenge on her father. Even if it killed him.

He thought, just then, that it might.

"Of course you're not," she said, and he thought that might be pity on *her* face. It set his teeth on edge. "It's all right, Chase. No need to go to such lengths to be an ass. I got the message."

She started toward him and something kicked at him, some bright shock of panic that she'd touch him and prove what a liar he was, or maybe it was only a flare of hope that she would—but then he realized he was standing next to the door, and she wasn't headed for him at all.

He told himself that was relief he felt, like a block of concrete inside him.

"In future," she said when she drew even with him, with dignity in her voice and every beautiful line of her stunning body, "you can simply say that you've changed your mind. No need for all these theatrics."

Chase said nothing as she walked past him and out into the hall. Nothing as she closed the door behind her with a gentle, admonishing sort of *click* instead of a great slam that might have indicated that she was as wrecked as he was—and therefore might have made him feel better. Nothing at all as she walked off down the hall, leaving him to his emptiness and his terrible shell, the lonely eyes he avoided in his mirror, his great hulking mausoleum and the dark maw of his regret.

A lifetime's worth of regret, piling higher all the time.

And nothing left inside him but his ghosts.

It was Chase's British accent that had made it so much worse, Zara decided a few days later while she indulged both her dark mood and her restlessness with a long, cold walk around the Whitaker estate. So much more eviscerating than if he'd said all the same things but had sounded as if he was from Weehawken, New Jersey, instead. It would have been embarrassing and upsetting either way, but with that accent of his, he'd been *withering*.

It played on a constant, deeply cutting cycle in her head.

You can't imagine you're the first woman to throw herself at me, can you?

It's not worth the bother.

And her personal favorite: *your sister offered me a blow job within five minutes of our introduction.*

He hadn't mentioned whether or not he'd accepted. Zara shoved her hands down as far as they'd go in her bulky winter coat and stamped harder against the path as she moved, because the crunch of ice and snow and frozen earth was primitively satisfying.

And because she was pretending it was his face.

His beautiful, terrible face, and those lonely eyes the perverse thing inside her still wanted to make better somehow. She was more than simply an idiot, Zara thought then. She was bordering on actively, unforgivably self-destructive.

Is this what you had in mind, Grams? she asked the fading light around her.

She puffed out a long breath, watching the cloud of it disappear in front of her, and scowled up at the massive house that reared up on the top of the barren hill, a dark and imposing silhouette against the night that was coming in too fast on a winter afternoon like this one, two days before Christmas.

A smart woman would have left this place—this marriage—after that scene in the dining room, she was forced to admit to herself, and yet here she was. Stomping about the estate half-frozen on another one of her solitary walks that neither cleared her head nor solved anything. But it was better than sitting in that bedroom suite that had started to feel a bit like a cell, pretending to work on her thesis when all she could think about was the man she knew was lurking about the rattling old house somewhere.

No doubt plotting out new ways to humiliate her.

It's not worth the bother. Your sister offered me a blow job.

"The facts are simple," she told herself then, out loud, as if that might banish that vicious loop from her head. She nestled her chin a bit farther into her favorite scarf, still glaring at the house and the lights in the windows, the sparkling Christmas trees and the soft strands of lights along the drive that made it all seem far more welcoming than it was. "You literally threw yourself at this man, and he rejected you." Her words were clouds against what remained of the daylight, but punched at her like heavy fists. "After kissing you like he thought he might die if he stopped."

That was the part she kept mulling over. The reversal.

If he'd simply rejected her outright, it might have been different, or so she'd told herself in these dark, chilly days since it happened, while he'd avoided her completely and she'd had nothing to do but brood about it. Zara hadn't reached the advanced age of twenty-six without having had her share of rejection. It was never pleasant, was it? Had Chase simply declined her offer, she liked to think she would have gracefully swallowed any stung pride and carried on—

Yeah, right.

She would have been mortified. She would have suffered through the rest of that dinner and then gone back to her room and prayed for immediate death, so she'd never have to face him again. But when the melodrama had passed, she would have been fine. Embarrassed, but fine.

If he'd rejected her in that snide, patronizing way but

without any kissing, Zara was fairly certain she would have walked out of that dinner, packed her things, called for a cab and taken herself back home to the little cottage that had once been her grandmother's in a pretty little village on Long Island Sound, where she could bundle herself up against the cold, light her own fire and hunker down for the long holiday break in peace and quiet. Chase could stay rude and obnoxious all on his own.

Because there was actually no reason that she and Chase had to stay together under one roof. Zara's life had always been wholly uninteresting to the entire world—no paparazzi dogged her every step, no curious neighbors took pictures of her on the sly and posted them on the internet. No one cared where she was, so she could pretend to be anywhere, couldn't she?

It was the kissing and *then* the rejection that she couldn't get past.

And only partly because calling what had happened *kissing* might have been technically accurate, but didn't come close to describing the experience.

Zara couldn't sleep. Or she did, only to wake gasping and burning up from the searing force of her dreams, all of which featured Chase. She *felt* him, that rangy body of his all around her, hard and hot and ready. That mouth of his, wicked and seductive in turn. The way he'd pulled her off that table and into his lap, like she was as light as a feather and as easily plucked from the air and then placed wherever he'd wanted her.

She'd never felt anything like it.

And she could still feel it now, she thought crossly, starting to move again because her feet had turned to blocks of ice inside her boots. Her chest was tight. Her breasts simply hurt, heavy and aching, while she could feel the thrust of her nipples against the fabric of her bra, abraded more with every step. And even as she made her way across the frozen lawn, up that hill toward the house, she could feel that desperate, molten heat between her legs.

All this from the *memory* of his hands on her, of that incandescent kiss, of his mouth like a joy and a curse on hers.

And there was absolutely no way that she could have imagined that he'd been as bowled over by it as she'd been. No way she'd fabricated the thunder of his heart in his chest, the way he'd held her head and her face like he'd never let her go, or God help her, the way he'd taken her apart every time he'd tasted her. Tormented her.

Taken her.

No way, she thought. That had all been real, despite what came after.

Zara trudged up to the top of the hill and then stopped, frowning, when she saw him through the tall, bright windows. She'd come up the north side of sloping lawn and that put her outside the farthest part of the house, where there was an indoor pool, a greenhouse atrium and a fitness area she kept telling herself she'd visit one of these days to work off Mrs. Calloway's cooking.

Chase was in the greenhouse, in the wide, central part surrounded by an explosion of well-tended tropical greenery, and at first she thought he was dancing.

He was so graceful. Smooth, athletic movement, one motion blending into the next, and it took her long moments to understand that he wasn't dancing at all—he was practicing some kind of martial art. She began to see kicks and strikes in the fluidity of his movements. That ruthless, formidable power of his exploding into a stream of controlled, yet lethal attacks.

But mostly, she saw *him*. Stripped bare to the waist and gleaming with the force of his exertions. Those haunted blue eyes of his and a sexily unshaven jaw, his dark hair much too long to be anything but wild. That he was truly the most beautiful man she'd ever beheld struck her square in the chest. Like one of his kicks.

Zara told herself it was her scholarly nature at work here. She liked research. She liked the compilation of facts, as many facts as she could find, no matter if she used them all or not in her final thesis. She liked to gather them and analyze them, then make her arguments.

This, she acknowledged as if from afar, was why she avoided "casual." Because she wasn't any good at it.

You're not delusional at all, she assured herself as she pushed open the greenhouse door and walked inside, stamping the cold off her boots and pretending not to notice that Chase froze in the middle of all those bright green plants and impossibly summery flowers, like she'd stepped through a portal to a different season altogether.

For a moment, they only stared at each other, and Zara was certain she could feel the weight of all that feral blue pressing into her, like the sudden embrace of the warm, soft air. She could hear the harsh sound of his breathing over the riot of her own pulse. Her skin prickled everywhere. Her cheeks were so hot she thought they might explode.

Then Chase shifted, breaking the connection. He turned his back on her and walked—stalked, really, in nothing but those loose black trousers that only seemed to call attention to the stark power he wore in every inch of those smooth, hard muscles—over to one of those heavy boxing bags that hung from its own metal apparatus that reminded Zara of the game hangman. And then he started to hit it. And kick it.

Hard.

Zara pulled her gloves off, one by one, then the wool hat from her head. She unwrapped her scarf from her neck, and then she shoved it all into her coat pockets. She unzipped her coat and shrugged it off, then tossed it all into a nearby chair, and while she had the kind of buzzing sensation in her ears and at the back of her neck that told her

Chase was perfectly aware of her throughout this whole process, he didn't stop beating the crap out of that bag.

And for some reason she felt every blow. Like he was landing them against her heart.

This is utter stupidity, she told herself. *And yes, delusional.*

But she didn't do any of the things she should have. She didn't leave. Not the room, not the house. She didn't hightail it back to her own life and to hell with what Chase thought, or her father thought. She didn't check herself into a nearby psychiatric institution to determine what madness this was that made her care what happened to this man.

That was the trouble, of course. She did care. Because this *was* her version of "casual," however pathetic. Married and yearning and caring, despite everything.

Because he looked tortured. That was what that particular wildness was this evening, pouring from him, filling the room like a scent. Like he was tearing himself apart the harder he hit that bag.

Like he was fighting his own demons with every punch he threw and every kick he landed. Fighting for his life.

Your sister offered me a blow job, he'd said. No doubt in precisely the way Zara had imagined Ariella would do such a thing. Zara wasn't about to compete with that. But she could offer something else. Something that had more to do with that stricken, compelling loneliness that shone so brightly in those eyes of his than with sex.

She wandered a little bit closer and then sat down on the little sofa that had been pushed back almost into the wall of plants, perhaps to make room for what she'd seen before and thought was dancing. She kicked off her boots and pulled her feet up under her.

And then she began to talk.

CHAPTER SIX

CHASE DIDN'T HAVE the slightest idea what she was on about.

The monster in him didn't care. It wanted her under him, not across the room, and who cared what happened to her when his New Year's Eve plan went off as intended? When he finally took his revenge? He wanted her, full stop. Now that she was breathing the same air as he was again, making him tight and hard and feral that easily, he couldn't understand the way he'd shoved her away that night at dinner. Much less the distance he'd kept from her since, no matter how many times Ben Calloway sang those vaguely romantic Christmas carols in his direction.

This is why, he told himself coldly. *Because you have no control where this woman is concerned.*

But that dark thing in him—sex and grief and hunger and need, heavy and fierce deep down into his bones until he couldn't tell who he was without it—didn't care.

He was so much more monster than he was man, and it appalled him. It made him hit the damned bag that much harder. And the more she talked, settling in on that couch as if they were great old friends and this was *comfortable,* the more he hit. The whole world narrowed down into those two things, like it was all part of the same great rhythm— her lovely voice, rich and warm, and the starkness of the violence he could dish out against inanimate objects he knew were merely stand-ins for him.

He was simply the instrument that linked the two, he told himself. And somehow, that made him feel less monstrous. Lighter. Warmer, the way she was so effortlessly.

"I look like my grandmother," Zara was saying, as conversationally as if he'd asked her. "She was Irish and always described herself as 'feisty,' though I never saw her do anything that wasn't strictly proper in that very old-money, patrician way. My father loathed her. She'd always liked his older brother much better than him, but Uncle Teddy died young. So when I ended up looking exactly like her, Dad transferred all of those feelings to me." Then she laughed, and it cascaded over him, sunbeams and heat. *Damn her.* "Or maybe that's what I decided to tell myself."

Chase had thought he'd finally lost it when she'd simply *appeared* at that door, in a rush of cold air and the darkening winter sky behind her. He thought he'd finally started seeing things, not merely the collection of familiar ghosts who usually cluttered his head.

He didn't know what to do with that scalding-hot, very nearly bright thing that had wound tight in him when he'd realized she was real. She was *here.* And despite what had happened between them the last time—what he'd done to her, he was well aware, because he couldn't seem to handle her the way he would any other woman—she appeared to be staying.

It couldn't be hope. Not that. He'd lost the last of his hope when he'd been thirteen. This was something different, he told himself grimly.

Because it had to be.

Chase hit the bag with his hands, his elbows, his knees, his feet. He hit and hit and hit, so hard he could feel the shock of it blasting through him, promising he'd regret it later when this raging thing in him wore off—but that only made him go harder. Faster. What *didn't* he regret?

Why should this, or anything that happened here, be any different?

He could still taste her. It was making him crazy.

Crazier, that was.

"My mother always claimed she was meant to be a great painter, but I think that was something she said to differentiate herself from the rest of the socialites she ran around with who had no aspirations beyond their weekly manicures."

Zara's voice had gone wry. Rueful, like she was crinkling up that fine nose of hers as she spoke, no doubt rendering herself dangerously adorable—but he would be damned if he'd look. Chase shuddered, imagining it anyway, and the heat that always graced those lovely cheeks of hers.

She was killing him.

"I never saw her paint a thing, but she picked fights with anyone who suggested that and hid from all the things she didn't feel like doing in the little guesthouse out back she called her studio. She used to lecture us about independence and personal freedom, but when she and my father finally divorced she demanded a laughably huge settlement. She lives on it to this day in her so-called 'artist's retreat' outside of Santa Fe with her collection of predatory boyfriends." A low, husky laugh that ripped at his self-control. "She doesn't encourage her grown daughters to visit her there, mind you. Or anywhere else. Predatory boyfriends require certain levels of care, maintenance and careful lies, and grown daughters make that a challenge, apparently. She claims she's still grieving the end of her marriage and seeing us only makes it worse. It's been five years."

Chase shifted, jumped up and down on the balls of his feet for a moment to recalibrate, then struck out with his knee. *Thunk.* And Zara's pretty voice rose and fell in the background, as thick and insistent around him as the humidity in the greenhouse. Making him sweat all the same. More.

Making him wish he could mete out a little justice to the people in her life the way he could to his punching bag.

Because you're such a hero, a derisive voice taunted him. *The perfect dispenser of truth and justice. What a laugh.*

He shifted again, then hit the bag with his elbow, hard enough to maim a real person, if never quite hard enough to silence his own demons.

"Ariella was the crowning achievement of my parents' marriage," Zara told him. "When we were growing up they would dress us alike and coo over her, telling her how pretty she was, how perfect, how cute. She was exactly the child they'd both secretly expected to have. Blonde and lovely and charming. Instantly beloved by anyone with eyes." Another low laugh, but this one was rougher, and he felt it like claws across his chest. "I was not."

Chase realized that growling sound was coming from him, and bit it back. So hard he almost bit off his own tongue.

"They sighed about my hair," she continued as if she hadn't heard him. "Which, in fairness, was more orange than red at the time. They told me to stand up straight, to walk softly, to be more careful and much more quiet. They hated when I called attention to myself in any way. Of course, that could mean when I walked into a room. It was hard to figure out the rules. And then it was worse when we were teenagers, because it wasn't only my parents saying those things."

But she didn't sound remotely self-pitying. She sounded faintly amused and analytical. And Chase found that hurt him. It *hurt*. Like a shot to the gut.

The bag rocked back and forth in front of him, like it was a balloon.

"But that's adolescence, isn't it? It's all wretched, unless you're pretty like Ariella and calculating enough to take advantage of it." That laugh again, which he was beginning to think might lodge itself in him forever, like permanent opiates in his bloodstream. What was wrong with him that he liked that idea? "I knew my place was in a book and I liked it there."

Thunk. Thunk.

But God help him, those greedy little noises she'd made, sprawled in his lap, her hot mouth wild against his. They haunted him. They woke him in the night. They kept him from his work. They'd wedged their way into him and made him ache for more.

He *ached*.

"My grandmother had always counseled me to give my family another chance. To let them see the real me. And when Ariella disappeared, I was the only one who could help," she told him, and he heard the change in her voice then. How serious it became, suddenly. "Me, at last. I could do something of value for my father that no one else could. It didn't matter that I knew exactly what kind of man he is. It didn't matter that I knew how unlikely it was that he'd ever see me as anything but a problem to solve. I could do the crazy thing that Ariella had walked away from. I know how pathetic that sounds, but for the first time in my whole life, he needed me. So I did it."

Chase stopped hitting the bag. There was an edginess in him, gnawing at the base of his spine, rushing through his veins. He was...affronted, he realized. That Amos Elliott should have that kind of power. That this woman should have spent a lifetime desperate for that petty little man's approval. That she was three-dimensional, *real*, and not the sort of easily digested and quickly dismissed woman

he'd been prepared to marry. There was no preparing for
Zara. She'd disarmed him from the start.

And Chase was very much afraid he didn't know who
he was without his weapons of choice.

He turned to look at her then, very slowly, and it was
worse than he'd thought. Much worse.

She was entirely too pretty, but she was also so *cute*.
He could have resisted a pouty display, a calculation of
curves and presentation. He could have resisted that particular cultivated attractiveness that passed for beautiful
in his circles, that he could hardly believe he'd accepted
all this time now that he'd seen this woman's perfect, in-
comparable glory. Now that he knew what she hid beneath
clothes that could never do her justice.

Zara sat cross-legged on the couch in dark corduroy
trousers and a cocoa-colored turtleneck sweater, her hair
in a careless sort of cascade all over her shoulders and not
a strand of it *orange*, her warm, pretty eyes gleaming gold
and soft. And that bloody mouth of hers that was the sexi-
est thing he'd ever tasted was so naked and so carnal, it
was like she was begging him to take it. *Her.* Taste it all
over again.

How could he defend against ghosts like her when she
wasn't a ghost at all? When she was real and *alive* and
here—*right here*—watching him with so much compas-
sion in her gaze that it stunned him? As surely as if she'd
landed a blow to the side of his head and left him spinning?

He had the disconcerting notion that she could see all
the way through him, to all that suffocating darkness he
carried within. And planned to keep talking to him until
he accepted it. Until he surrendered to this inept bridge
she was building between them with these stories of hers,
like the two of them were at all the same.

He knew better.

Anyone else would have kept their distance from him

when he was like this, so obviously on the edge of un-hinged. Chase knew that. And yet here she sat, looking wholly unintimidated, telling him these stories about her life. Making him *understand* her the way he imagined people did when they weren't the kind of broken he was. When they were getting to know each other in all those ways he assumed normal people must.

When they hadn't killed their own mother and knew better, therefore, than to risk any more bridges or connections. He knew how these things ended.

But there was something like a howl in him, long and deep and shattering. Chase hurt everywhere, from the bag and from her and from *this thing* he couldn't seem to banish. Much less control.

And he didn't know what he meant to do with this woman—he didn't know how to make her his revenge when he couldn't seem to make her do anything, but he couldn't take *this* any longer. He couldn't stand it.

"I'm not empty inside," he blurted out, gravel and steel in his voice, and she jerked in her seat as if he'd smacked her. He hated himself as if he really had.

"What?"

But he was already crossing the room. He was already right there, looming above her, so obviously brutal and dangerous, and yet she still gazed up at him in a kind of wonder. Like she saw all the things in him he'd stopped wishing were there a long, long time ago.

Like she was as much a fool as he was.

"It's much worse than empty in here," he rasped. "It's a murderous dark, vicious and *wrong*, and there's no changing it. You should have run away from me when I gave you the chance, Zara. You should have understood that it was a gift, and I don't know that I'll hand you another one."

Her eyes had gone wide, but her chin tipped up, in another show of spine and determination he couldn't understand. What was wrong with this woman? She saw too much, much more than anyone else he'd let near him in years—so why wasn't she afraid of him the way she should have been?

"So is this," she said. "Do you think I sit around and tell people my life story, Chase? In all its sad little details? I don't generally like to hand people ammunition when I know that sooner or later, they're going to use me as target practice."

He didn't deny it. He saw the knowledge of that in the way she tightened her lips, but she still didn't look away.

"I told you I would ruin you." He watched her swallow hard, and he didn't know what it was about that, why it flashed over him like a wave of heat. "You should have listened."

He sank down on his knees before her, fascinated by the way she flushed. By her slight jerk against the couch, as if she'd had to wrestle herself into submission to keep herself from leaping out of her own skin. He held her gaze as he leaned forward and stuck a fist on either side of her, one at each lush hip.

And then they were close again. Much too close. It was like baiting a tornado, daring it to touch land, and the roar of it filled him. *Need. Lust.* And that other thing that couldn't be hope, not even its battered and bruised cousin, but moved in him nonetheless.

"I listened." Her voice was only slightly breathy, but he felt it as if she'd taken him deep in her mouth. The ache. The sweet burn. "You were as hideous as possible, to be certain I would. But what I don't understand is why."

"I told you why. In detail."

His voice was grittier. Darker. And he was leaning over her, his mouth the scantest breath from hers, and she didn't have to call him a liar. She didn't have to say a word. He was proving it.

But this was Zara. She smirked at him.

"You told me *something* in detail," she agreed. "But I'm not sure I would call that little performance an explanation. Would you?"

Chase decided he might as well take this collision course he was on—that they were both on and he didn't understand how that had happened—to its logical conclusion. Or go insane.

More insane.

But he couldn't care about that the way he knew he should. She was so *lush* and she was breathing too hard, and he could see the flush of arousal tint her cheeks pink. He could smell the delicate scent of her skin, like gardenias and vanilla, and he felt it wrap around him like a noose.

Chase gave up. He stopped fighting and let the monster take control, dark and greedy and wild.

He leaned in and slammed his mouth to hers.

It was like fireworks. Everywhere.

Inside her, around her.

Zara couldn't breathe. She didn't care that she couldn't. She wound her arms around his strong neck as his hands wrapped over her hips and tugged her closer. She dropped her legs to either side of him, and he surged between them as if he belonged there, until she locked her ankles behind him.

And then they were finally plastered together, her aching breasts flat against the wall of his chest, like she'd been crafted to fit against him just like that. She could feel him between her legs, the smooth, solid heft of his finely wrought form, and she shook with a ravenous hunger she'd never, ever felt before. Sensation washed over her, blowing out all her circuits and then lighting them up again, leaving her shaking and greedy and as wild as he felt against her.

This wasn't a kiss. This wasn't anything so sweet.

This was possession. Raw and intense.

And she had never wanted anything more.

He tasted of salt and need, passion and demand. And she couldn't get enough.

"More," he muttered against her mouth, and then he pulled back from her.

This was when clarity should have asserted itself, Zara thought, as he took her legs from around him and set her feet back on the floor. But then he looked at her, that dark, impossible blue gone brilliant with need, and she didn't care if she survived this. She didn't care what happened next, so long as it did.

Just so long as he didn't stop this time.

It was as if he could read her mind. His surprisingly tough hands, more laborer than CEO, and she assumed it was the martial arts that made them that way, went to the waistband of her trousers. Zara's heart walloped at her, and her own hands met his there—but to help him or to stop him? She didn't know.

"Take them off." It was an order, and he didn't pretend otherwise. Not with that stark, nearly guttural tone of voice. Not with that shattering look in his eyes that didn't look in the least bit lonely now. They looked hot.

White-hot and focused directly on her.

Zara pulled open the top button of her trousers. Her mouth had gone dry, and she licked her lips before she thought better of it, and then her breath stuttered when his gaze moved to her mouth, dark and hungry.

"Did you accept?" she asked before she knew she meant to say something. It took a long time for him to find his way from her mouth, and he'd gone that much wilder when he did. He was taut and hard. She was almost shaking from the sheer insanity of being this close to him, this *hot*, this eternally *hungry*, and seeing the same reflected in every line of his beautiful face. "My sister's lovely offer. When you met."

He looked blank for a long, deeply satisfying moment. Then his expression went feral. Calculating in a purely sensual, ruthless sort of way that shouldn't have thrilled her as fully as it did, sweeping through her like light.

"Would it matter if I had?"

More than it should, she realized. She wished she hadn't asked.

"I've made it a strict policy to avoid going where Ariella has forged any kind of path," Zara told him, fighting to keep her voice smooth and even dry, though she wasn't sure she succeeded. "Be that a favored vacation spot, a neighborhood in a city, a room in the same house. A man. It helps avoid any confusion."

Chase laughed. It skittered over her skin, then lodged itself in all of her tender places. Her nipples thrust toward him. Her core tensed and then melted. She shivered. And he'd never looked so wicked, so dangerously sexy, as when he leaned close again and spread his hands out over her belly that she hadn't known until that moment had been revealed when her sweater rode up.

His palms were hot and faintly coarse against her skin, and he simply held them there for a moment, his gaze narrow and something like amused on hers, and she hated that he could feel her quiver. That he could feel the goose bumps that rose all over her at the fiercely possessive way he held his hands there.

She hated it. She thought she'd die if he stopped.

"Is this confusion?" It was a taunt, and so it shouldn't have worked through her like liquid heat. "Because it rather feels like something else."

"Like avoiding the question, you mean?"

He blinked, and as she always did, Zara got the impression she'd surprised him. That most people didn't speak to this man this way, as if he was something other than lethal and untamable. She wished she could read the light that moved through those eyes of his, then over his remarkable face.

He laughed again. Low and something like indulgent. Then, inexorably, as if he'd never intended to do anything but this from the start, he shifted closer. He twisted one hand around and stroked his way beneath her half-opened trousers.

Zara jolted. Chase knew exactly what he was doing. His fingers found her latest thong covering her and stroked inside, slicking through her folds and then holding her there for a molten instant, hot and wet and in his hand.

"Does it matter?" he asked again, low and too close to her ear, while his fingers began to move. Learning her. Testing her. Then thrusting inside her. "Do you mind where I've been?"

Zara's mind blanked out. There was nothing but the hard hand that wrapped around one hip and held her still and that other one, that wicked one that was breaking her apart with every slick, easy thrust. With the sure pressure of his palm against her center while he used two fingers to drive her up, then up further, then into dizziness.

"If I say yes, will you turn me away?" he whispered, daring her, and then he laughed again. "Right now?"

He did something magical with his hand, a hard, sweet twist, and then Zara was gone. Shattered, that easily and that completely. Thrown apart into so many blissful pieces she was terrified she'd never come back—

But she did.

Eventually, she did, and he was waiting. Watching. That heavy hand still holding her core, his blue eyes intent on her face and dangerously, heart-thumpingly wild.

"No," he grated at her, fierce and low. "I never touched your sister. She never touched me. I'm not a pig."

She was still shivering through the aftershocks, and she couldn't speak. She thought there was an echo still bouncing around the glass in this atrium, and she was terribly afraid it was her. Screaming. Possibly even his name. She watched his mouth twist and that darkness move over his face, and she felt the tension in him them, in all the places they touched.

"Chase…" she managed to say, though she didn't know where she meant to go afterward.

"I warned you," he muttered.

And then he moved again. He dispensed with her trousers in a certain, shocking economy of motion that had them down her legs and whisked aside before she could draw a full breath.

"I'm not a good man, Zara," he told her, but the look on his face was bright and greedy, and he was staring down at the scrap of multicolored lace between her legs. "But if I don't taste you, I think I might die."

And like that, the fire swept through her again, tossing her right back into the heat of it. His gaze locked onto hers as he moved, tugging her bottom forward until it was on the edge of the sofa cushion, then crouching down to press her thighs open with the breadth of his shoulders. Her hands were somehow sunk in the rough black silk of his hair, and she didn't know how that had happened or why she seemed to be completely incapable of letting go of him.

And she was trembling. Everywhere.

"I don't think this is a good idea," Zara whispered.

And he grinned at her, this stunning creature, all raspy jaw and wild blue eyes, his mouth so close to her core that she was sure he could hear the way her pulse beat there. Or taste it.

"I know it's not," he agreed.

And then he pushed her thong aside and licked his way into her.

Zara simply *ignited*.

Thought fell away. There was nothing but Chase and the hungry way he feasted on her. He used his tongue like a weapon and she was helpless before it. She shook. She broke apart. She spun and she spun, and he only pushed her higher. Further. Deeper.

And when she convulsed around him this time, she heard a high, keening sound, and she didn't care that it was her. She only wondered how the glass around them didn't shatter. How the night simply hung there outside the windows without rending itself apart.

When she could move, she found she was limp and soft, sprawled back against the couch with her legs where he'd left them, tremors still chasing themselves across her skin.

She smiled before she thought better of it, wide and sleepy, and only then did she really look at Chase.

He'd sat back, lounging on the floor before the couch in a lazy way that was belied by every tight, hard line of his body and the intent way he watched her. Ruthless and hungry. Waiting. There should have been some kind of power in sitting higher than him, Zara thought, but he was too formidable for that. She doubted it would matter if he'd knelt there before her with his forehead to the floor; he was the least docile creature she'd ever seen. She thought of great, wild animals then, all with that contained force and the same predatory gaze.

Chase didn't move. He watched. And the more the silence grew heavy, the more Zara felt it like a fist in her belly. Hard and impossible to ignore.

She struggled to sit up, then looked around for her trousers, feeling a whole spinning host of things she really, really didn't want to feel. She decided to ignore them. She picked up the tangled pile of corduroy from the floor and stood, stepping into them and pulling them back up.

And all the while he lounged there, reminding her of a great big, indolent cat. Except far less cuddly.

"Let me guess," she said when her trousers were fastened, her cheeks flared so hot she thought she might run back out into the cold outside to relieve them and she was reasonably certain her voice wouldn't quake when she spoke. "This was a mistake. You wouldn't want to confuse me, as that will make me tumble straight off the cliff and find myself violently in love with you. You can get sex anywhere, Ariella was hotter, you're not really that interested." She smiled again, but this one was sharp enough to leave marks. "See? I listen."

He lifted himself up from the floor and onto his feet in a single, smooth jump that made her blink. Then clench hard, deep inside. Lethal grace. Impossible beauty.

She was in so far over her head with this man it was a wonder she could breathe at all, and the worst part was, she could still *feel* him. That talented mouth of his, like he was still licking heat into the core of her.

"Come," he muttered, short and dark. *Pissed off*, if she'd had to characterize it.

"I have to tell you," she said, because she couldn't seem to help herself. "If this is all part of some plot to put me in my place by punishing me with oral sex, I have to say, it's..." She paused when his gaze slammed into hers, looking somehow amused and furious at once. She swallowed. "Working, obviously. I feel very, very punished."

He muttered something else she couldn't hear, though it moved over her like his hard, capable hands. Then he jerked his head, bidding her precede him out of the greenhouse and back into the main house. The halls felt drafty and cool after the close heat of the atrium, and she felt it slap against the flush she knew must have turned her bright red.

Chase stalked beside her, his face shut down and forbidding and those blue eyes glittering brighter than the twenty-foot Christmas tree that dominated the front hall. He escorted her in that same tense silence all the way up to her suite, then stopped.

"Thank you," she said brightly, only half-aware that she was poking at him. And then unable to stop herself when she realized it. "That was fun. Especially the angry walking through the gloomy house. I think that part was my favorite."

He shifted, making Zara aware that her back was to the door and he was very big, very male, and not looking at her in any way that a wise woman would ignore. Or poke at any further.

But as she had proved a number of times already in her two and a half weeks of arranged marriage with this man, she was anything but wise where he was concerned.

"I am going to have a shower," he told her, and she had the sense he was biting off each word carefully. Like he couldn't trust they wouldn't simply run away with him if he wasn't vigilant. Or like he was *this close* to acting on that dark heat she could see shading his gaze, turning that wild blue something nearer to slate. "A very cold one. And then I'll meet you for the evening meal, as usual."

"None of this seems to end well," she pointed out. "Maybe we should stop trying. There's no law that says we have to cohabitate, you know."

"Don't tell me any more stories, Zara." His voice was low. Not quite angry, though; it was too quiet for that—and somehow he was closer than he should have been. "You don't want to win me over. I'm no kind of prize, I assure you. More like something you'd be better off endeavoring to avoid at all costs."

But he reached over and took a long, red wave of her hair in his fingers as he said it, then stared at it for a moment too long as he wrapped the shining strands around his finger. He shifted that stare to her when he tugged, not as gently as he could have done. The stare or the tugging.

"Are you sure about that?" She was whispering as if it hurt, though it didn't. Or not acutely, anyway.

"I am." He let go of her hair, and Zara felt bereft when he stepped back, like he'd taken all the heat and light with him. It was gone from his gaze as if it had never been. "Utterly, painfully sure."

And when he turned abruptly and stalked off down the hall, she stood there for too long, watching him until he disappeared into his own rooms—and told herself that what she felt then was relief.

CHAPTER SEVEN

IT WAS RELIEF because it couldn't be anything else, Zara told herself staunchly as she marched inside her room and started peeling off her clothes. Certainly not longing. Or anything like disappointment.

You should be relieved that someone *in this absurdity of a marriage managed to keep his wits about him,* a caustic voice inside of her snapped. *What were you thinking?*

But that was the trouble. She'd never thought less in her life. Her brain didn't appear to be involved at all when it came to Chase—and Zara hardly knew how to process that revelation. Thinking had always been her refuge. Her escape. Her single and best weapon.

She kicked her trousers off and surveyed the damage—none of it in her thoughts, which careened madly this way and that and offered nothing in the way of solace. She felt tremulous and still a scalding kind of tender between her legs. Her knees seemed wobbly, as if she might topple over at any moment and then crumple to the floor like the turtleneck sweater she swept over her head and then dropped at the foot of her bed. Her breasts ached, her nipples still pushed out taut and hard, and she had no idea why she couldn't seem to control herself where Chase was concerned.

Or why some part of her didn't *want* to control herself.

"Whatever made you think you could wade in and handle him?" she asked herself out loud as she made her way to the sprawling bathroom suite and turned on the water in the large, glassed-in shower. It fell from two separate fixtures like rain. "You can't handle yourself."

Zara knew that if she worried over it too much more, she'd explode. So instead, she stepped into the shower and let the heat pound into her. She stood under the spray with her head tipped back and gave herself up to the water. She could have stood there forever.

There were far worse places to hide, if only from herself. Eventually, the water would run cold. And maybe by then she'd have figured out how she could ever trust her own judgment again. Maybe she'd even wash herself clean of all that leftover sensation—

But then the glass door opened, the cooler air gusting in from outside the stall like ice against her heated skin.

She jerked out of the spray, startled if not precisely surprised, as Chase stepped into the glass enclosure. Big and male, formidable and still so beautiful, even while he made the huge shower stall seem puny around him.

His face was drawn. Harsh and intent. His gaze burned. He still wore those exercise trousers of his, but he didn't seem to care when the hot water soaked them on contact.

Zara knew she should say something. *Do* something.

But instead she merely stood there, caught as surely as if he'd trapped her between his hands and held her fast. As no small part of her wished he would.

She took a deep, shuddering breath. It did nothing at all to calm her.

"I can't seem to help myself," he grated at her, sounding aggrieved and somewhat accusing. "I've broken every last one of my rules with you already."

Zara blinked. "I'm sorry."

She didn't know why she'd said that, when she was a great many things indeed and not one of them was *sorry*, but she knew that hard curve in his lethal mouth was all for her. Maybe that was all the *why* she needed.

"I believe you will be, Zara, and far sooner than you think. But we are both doomed here. Never doubt it."

He moved closer, taking more of the spray on his wide, strong shoulders, and Zara's whole world shrank down to this. *Him.* His reckless blue gaze. His hard mouth. His inky-black hair wet against his head. The water coursing down his long, lean torso, highlighting the flat, hard planes of his chest and the ridged abdomen beneath, all of it dusted with a smattering of dark hair.

That haunted, hungry look on his face.

Again, she didn't think. She slapped her hands against the wall of his pectoral muscles and ignored the jolt of heat that rebounded back into her palms, arrowing directly into her core.

"Don't start," she told him, fearless in her need. If that was what was pounding in her like a drum, incessant and much too loud. A hot, molten pulse. "Not if you plan to stop again. I can't take the whiplash."

He ignored her hands. He simply leaned toward her despite them, took her face between his callused palms, and then his mouth was on hers, deep and wild. All of that volcanic heat. All of that terrible, wonderful fire.

Zara wanted to do nothing at all but burn.

"I'm not going to stop," he said against her mouth, a gruff and hungry thing that shook all the way through her and lit her up, from sex to scalp and back again. "I can't. But I can't make you any promises about whiplash."

She was wet again, flushed and pretty and red. She was hot and slippery from the water, like a thousand fantasies. And she still tasted too damned good. It wound in him, kicking over barriers and knocking down walls, and all he could do was angle his jaw for a better fit and keep right on kissing her.

This was a terrible idea.

Chase knew it.

He'd known it when he'd stood in his own bedroom, trying to breathe deep and ignore the imperative voice inside him that urged him to turn around and go back to her. To finally get her beneath him, above him, whatever. To sink deep inside her and who cared how?

He'd known it with every step he took down that long hall, and he'd certainly known it when he stood there in that bathroom again, staring at the indistinct impression of her lovely naked body on the other side of the steamed glass. He'd watched her, head tipped back, arms wrapped around her middle, and he could have left then with her none the wiser. He'd stopped his forward momentum, after all. He'd thought better of what he was about to do, and he'd known, with every last fiber in his being, that it was a mistake.

And he'd still walked straight into that shower.

It was a terrible idea that he would deeply regret, he knew as he pulled back. He held her to him, that luscious body flush against his at last, her bright gold eyes slumberous, the water making her glorious hair dark beneath his hands. It was among the worst ideas he'd ever had.

But it didn't stop him backing her up until she was against the tiled wall and he was angling into her, holding her fast, pressing himself against the particular beauty of her heavy breasts.

"You should stop this now," he told her, gritting the words out, sounding almost as if he was angry. Maybe he was. "You should run while you can. You've no idea the things I'm capable of doing to you."

She blinked, and then her sunset eyes gleamed in a way that went straight to his groin.

"Perhaps we'd better stop, then," she agreed, her voice perfectly sweet but that clever slap beneath. The undoing of him, and he suspected she knew it. "The way you're carrying on, anything that follows can only be a disappointment, don't you think? There is such a thing as over-selling, Chase."

"I'm trying to protect you," he growled. She didn't know who he was. She didn't know what he was capable of doing, what he'd done when he was still a kid—

She rolled her eyes. Evidently unimpressed.

Chase stared. He racked his brain and couldn't think of the last time anyone had dared.

"At this point I'm verging on bored," Zara said, moving her hips in a decidedly suggestive manner against him. He blew out a harsh breath between his teeth and tried to keep that great, dark thing in him leashed. "All you've done is stop when I want to go on and mutter dire threats about dark and terrible things you never quite name. Oh, and insult me. Lest we forget."

"You should be more wary then. I sound remarkably unstable."

"You don't know much about psychology, do you?" she asked, and her eyes were shining then, that little quirk in her lips so magnetic, so delicious, he didn't know if he wanted to lick it or test it with his teeth. "The single best way to get someone to walk down a dark and scary hallway is to moan and wail and issue a thousand warnings about how important it is they never, ever do exactly that."

"I am not a dark hallway," he told her. "But that doesn't mean I won't hurt you."

"Otherwise known as Pandora's box," she continued blithely. "At the bottom of which was hope, I believe. I think I'll survive, Chase. Assuming you ever stop with all the threats and warnings and dark mutterings and *do something*."

His hands tightened. He fought a thousand battles inside himself and lost them all.

"Show me a little self-preservation, Zara. That's all I ask."

"I'm fresh out." But she stretched her arms up and looped them around his neck, arching all of those delectable curves into him, making him nearly shake with the effort of controlling himself, however tenuously. Her smile went wicked and shot through him like flame. "I'm beginning to suspect that you can't deliver."

He stared at her for a moment, then laughed.

It was a real laugh, and he wasn't sure when that had last happened. Her eyes were warm on him and filled with mischief, and the laughter moved through him fast, lighting him up and fusing with all of that need and hunger. Turning into something much more potent.

He was still laughing when he kissed her again, and it made everything that much more intense. It rocketed through him, turning him to fire. Making him wild. Desperate.

Finally, he slid his hands up the tempting curve of her waist and found her breasts. He tore his mouth from hers and looked down as he held them in his hands at last, and then he bent to pull one taut nipple into his mouth.

She moaned and bucked against him, and that made it better. He felt an answering bolt of lust in his sex. He learned the shape of her breasts, their texture, each proud ridge. He played with them, using his hands and his mouth and the faint edge of his teeth, until she was thrashing against him, her cheeks that scarlet he craved and her mouth soft and open.

Her skin was like satin, and he wanted to taste every inch of it. He pulled back from her, and her eyes fluttered open, dazed and soaked through with a delicious, decadent heat that he could feel roaring in every part of him.

"My turn," she whispered.

Chase let her push him back to the other wall of the shower and watched intently as she followed, pressing red-hot kisses along his neck and then lower to find and tease each of his own nipples. She kept going, sinking to her knees before him as she kissed and licked and tortured him, following the line of dark hair that led across his stomach and down beneath his too-wet, now much too heavy trousers.

Zara reared back on her heels and glanced up at him, and that tiny little smile curved over her mouth. She held his gaze as she reached out and shoved the trousers down over his hips, freeing him at last, and then she pulled them all the way to the floor of the shower.

Chase kicked them aside, but Zara was focused on him. On his sex, which was so close to her mouth it made it impossible for him to breathe normally.

"Finally," she murmured, which went straight to his head, far more potent than any whiskey.

She looked up at him again, and he felt his heart give a great kick inside his chest, and then she simply leaned forward and took his length deep in her mouth.

He thought he died.

Her mouth was hot and lascivious. Perfect. She reached out and took hold of him, using her hands along with her mouth and setting a lazy, devastating rhythm that Chase thought might be the undoing of him.

He had no intention of moving, but his hands sank into her hair, to keep himself grounded in the reality of her more than to guide her, and still she kept on, licking and sucking him, worshipping him, turning him inside out with every deft sweep of her tongue.

Maybe she wasn't the only one who should have been wary, he thought—

And then realized that he was an instant away from embarrassing himself.

"No," he managed to say, in a stranger's voice. "Not like this."

He hauled her up against him, slapping the water off with his free hand and then simply lifting her into his arms.

The effect on Zara, who had been nearly unflappable thus far in their brief acquaintance, was nothing short of electric.

She went pale, then stinging red, and her entire body went stiff.

"You can't *carry* me!" she hissed at him.

Chase frowned at her. He shouldered his way out of the shower stall, holding her high against him as he strode into the bedroom.

"Are you sure?" he asked. "Because I appear to be doing it."

"No, it's just— You can't— I'm too—" But whatever it was she wanted to say, she couldn't seem to get it out.

He stopped beside the bed with her still in his arms and studied her face.

"Had I known this was all it took to unsettle and silence you, I would have picked you up in the damned church," he said drily.

"You'll give yourself a hernia," she snapped at him, temper in her eyes and mortification splashed over her cheeks and down her chest.

And finally, the penny dropped.

Chase laughed. He placed her on the bed and climbed up with her, rolling them over to the center of the mattress so she was on her back and he could look down into that lovely pink face of hers. She was scowling at him as if she was furious, but he could see now what lurked behind it.

"You are perfect," he told her with absolute sincerity.

Her scowl only deepened. "I've told you before that I

don't like being patronized. I'll add to that the fact I *really* don't like it when I'm naked."

"You should always be naked," he muttered, shifting so he could press his mouth to the place where her pulse went wild in her neck. "Clothes do you a grave disservice. You have the body of a lost goddess and I intend to taste every last inch of it."

"Chase." Her voice was so taut, so constricted, he stopped what he was doing and looked up. Her eyes were big and too dark, and they searched his almost hesitantly. "I'm not the sort of woman men pick up and carry places."

He propped himself up on one elbow and traced a finger down her lovely neck, then around one breast, fascinated by the soft slope of it and the blush that stained her there, too. He could feel the shiver that worked through her, and it made the fire in him burn hotter.

"I didn't realize there was a particular type of woman suitable for lifting," he said. "They're not free weights or barbells, are they? But there are certainly a large number of weak men roaming about, it has to be said. I'm not sure they could pick up a scone if pressed to do so, much less a grown woman."

"I stood up in the bath on the first night I was here—"

"Believe me, Zara. That is not something I am ever likely to forget."

"—so that we could dispense with these games. I don't need the seduction routine." She frowned at him. "I know what I look like. I know what every woman you've ever been photographed with looks like. I know that by your standards, I'm a fat cow." Her chin lifted, and he almost believed that blazing thing in her gaze. Almost. "And don't you dare argue with me. I'm *fine* with it."

His brows rose, as much in amazement that she could be so wrong as any kind of challenge. "Evidently not."

"I'd prefer it if you'd stop pretending I'm interchangeable with Ariella," she threw at him. "It's demeaning to all of us."

He couldn't help himself. He laughed again, and she let out a sound that might well have been a curse and started to roll away from him. Chase moved over her, pinning her beneath him with his lower body and his hands on either side of her furious face, and made no effort to hide his arousal.

"Zara." He waited until she looked at him, her golden eyes too bright. "What terrible lies have you been telling yourself?"

"It's the truth," she whispered. "As I told you earlier. It was made clear to me a very long time ago."

He ran his thumbs over her marvelous cheekbones, studied the weight of the dark lashes that rimmed those gorgeous eyes of hers.

"You told me that your father is even more of an ass than I'd imagined, your mother is a rather sad narcissist, and I already know your sister is cruel and vapid," he said, and he didn't know himself then. He didn't understand where this was coming from, this patient thing in him that felt too much like kindness. *As if she matters*, a voice intoned, *and more than simply as an agent of revenge*. He couldn't acknowledge it. He refused. "Why should it matter what such people think of you? Why on earth should you accept what they call truths?"

She moved, some kind of restlessness or even panic, but she didn't try to shove him off her, and that same strange thing in him he couldn't bring himself to look at too closely called that a victory.

"I don't need the strange man I married, who I hardly know and who hasn't been particularly nice to me anyway, to tell me pretty little lies so I'll sleep with him," she rasped, emotion high on her cheeks and a matching heat in her gaze. "I came to terms with reality a long time ago. I might have a childish yearning to please my dead grandmother and my eternally disapproving father, but never fear, I'm aware of how problematic that is. And how unlikely it is I'll ever be successful. I certainly don't need you to pretend I'm beautiful on top of all that. It's insulting."

Chase felt something inside of him break free then. Dissolve, like ice in warm water, and he understood that the danger this woman posed was far greater and far deeper than he'd already imagined.

But he shut down that line of thought, because it could only lead to all those dark places he didn't want to visit. Not here. Not now.

Not when he still thought he might die if he didn't find a way inside her.

"You are beautiful," he said bluntly. "Stunning, in fact."

She made a furious sort of noise. "You're *ruining* this!"

"I beg your pardon?"

"I don't understand why this is happening to me," she said in a sort of moan, as if complaining to the ceiling above them. Then she turned that glare on him. "You're supposed to be the kind of man who somersaults in and out of random women's beds like you're auditioning for the circus. Why can't we just have sex? Why is there all this *talking*?"

He shook his head, astounded. Again. And that thing inside of him spread, gaining ground like he was the same as any other man. Like he could do this kind of thing without collateral damage. Without losing himself and destroying her—and everything else he touched—in the process.

But none of that mattered. Not now. Not while he was pressed against her slippery, naked body, at last. Not while he had the whole night to show her exactly how wrong she was.

He couldn't wait.

"I'm not going to argue about this, Zara," he told her, a low, dark thread of sound that he could *see* wind its way through her. "If you can't process the truth when it's offered, the least you can do is shut up, lie back and let me prove it to you."

She stared back at him. He smiled. "Now."

Zara meant to argue the point. But Chase merely shifted back and dropped his head to her breast, licking his way to her nipple and pulling it deep into his mouth.

And somehow, as the wildfire seized her, she forgot.

To fight. To make him admit that she was too big, too unattractive, too *much*, as she'd always been told. As she'd accepted she was, because that was the only thing that made any sense out of how she'd been treated her whole life.

She could still taste him on her tongue—the sheer, dizzying maleness of him, the strength and the soft steel. She hadn't wanted to stop, kneeling there before him as the hot water poured over them both, cocooning them in all that heated sensation. She'd wanted to keep going until he was as weakened by this madness as she felt. She'd wanted to drown in him, then do it all over again.

And then he'd picked her up like she was as light as air. Her whole world had shot straight out of its orbit that easily, leaving her hurtling through space and light-headed from the speed of it.

Chase shifted again, letting one hand smooth its way down over her belly to cup her femininity beneath, and Zara forgot all of that, too.

There was nothing but the way he kissed her, trailing fire and hunger from one breast to the other, then the valley between, making her breath catch. There was nothing but his clever hand at her very core, tracing her and teasing her, testing that proud center and then sliding deep inside of her, until she was thrashing beneath him, so close yet again—

"Look at you," he murmured in her ear, so dark and so

ruthlessly masculine she shivered. "I've never seen any-thing so beautiful in the whole of my life."

"Stop saying that," she managed to get out, but he was moving again. He settled himself between her legs, his heavy shaft taking the place of his fingers. And then he waited, propped up over her and poised at her entrance, while every part of her screamed and shook.

"When you stood up in that bath the first night, I lost the power of speech," he told her, and *his voice*. She thought it might ruin her, the way it moved in her and made her shake.

"I wish you would now." She tried to pull him in, her legs at his hips, her hands at his waist, but he only laughed and stayed where he was. "What kind of careless, selfish playboy are you? We should have had sex five times by now. This is like torture."

"I haven't begun to torture you," he assured her with that wondrous dark thing in his voice that swept over her like some kind of honey. "You won't have to wonder, Zara. You'll know. I'm quite inventive."

"Let's hope that in the meantime I don't die of bore-dom, then," she threw at him, and he laughed again in that maddening way that she thought might make her scream out her frustration in earnest—

And then he simply thrust into her, deep and hard.

Slick. Intense.

Perfect.

He was big everywhere but it didn't hurt, it simply made her *aware*. That he was deep inside her. As if he'd been made for precisely this. As if she had.

He wasn't laughing anymore. His chest was moving like he was running a race, and his beautiful face had gone stark with the same need that pounded in her. His blue eyes blazed with hunger.

He slid out, then thrust again, and they both groaned.

The whole world fell away. Chase moved over her, gathering her closer to him as he set a shattering rhythm. Zara dug her hands into his smooth, hard flesh and met him, stroke after stroke, surrendering herself completely. Letting the dark thrill take her over.

Letting him take her wherever he wanted to go.

And the irony was, as she met each glorious thrust, as they moved together in a new sort of grace they built there between them, she had never felt more beautiful in her life.

This is where you belong, something kept whispering, like a chant in her ear. *At last. Right here.*

Chase started to move faster. Deeper. He ran a hand down her side, then to the center of her need and circled it. Teasing—but he couldn't continue in that vein for long. She felt the shudder move over him and knew he was as torn apart as she was. As raw.

He pressed down hard, and she was lost. That easily.

She shook around him, crying out his name, and he drank it in with a feral growl against her shoulder. And before she could recover herself, before she could come back down, he dug beneath them to hold her bottom in his hands and cradled it.

Then he thrust into her. Harder. Deeper. Far more demanding and so good, so *perfect*, it threw her straight back into the dancing flames and then over that edge again.

And this time, when she fell off into that sweet oblivion, he followed.

Later, Zara came awake in a sudden rush, aware instantly that she was alone.

Of course you're alone, that nasty little voice inside her that sounded a great deal like her sister snapped. *What did you expect?*

She sat up slowly, almost afraid to take stock of what she felt in the aftermath. She shoved the great mess of her

hair back from her face and looked around the room instead, absurdly—perhaps disastrously—touched by the
fact he'd lit the fire before he'd left. It crackled and danced,
throwing light all around, and its sheer exuberance made
her feel better.

More like the creature Chase had claimed she was than
the one she knew, deep down, she truly was.

It was a deep, inky dark outside her windows, and she
wasn't at all surprised to see that it had got late. That it
was Christmas Eve, technically, and she couldn't help her
small smile at that. They'd come together twice more in
that bed, rolling and laughing and driving each other mad,
before she'd fallen into an exhausted slumber.

If it never happened again, she told herself stoutly, she'd
be fine. *Perfectly fine.*

But she felt herself turn crimson anyway, her body calling her a liar. Or, worse, an addict.

She moved to the edge of the bed and pulled herself to
standing with a hand on one of the four posts, letting her
bare feet hit the chilly floor. Zara shivered and hurried her
way across the cold expanse to her walk-in closet. She was
reaching for her heaviest pair of winter socks when she
heard the door open behind her in the main room.

Chase, she saw when she poked her head out of the
closet. A scowling, half-naked Chase, who was holding a
tray of food, which Zara found about as unlikely as she'd
have found the appearance of a Christmas elf.

For a long moment, they stared at each other.

"Don't dress on my account," he growled at her, and
then stalked over to the low table in front of the fire and
slapped the tray down.

Zara pulled on the nearest things she could find—a
pair of lounging trousers and a soft, cashmere sweater on
top—and, after a brief and vicious internal struggle that

was all about the vanity she'd thought she'd eradicated years before, the ugly socks, as well.

"You brought food?" she asked as she walked over to the couch where he waited, standing there in front of the fire and *glaring*.

"Is that a question or a statement of fact?"

"A simple *yes* or *no* would have sufficed, for future reference, Mr. Grouchy All The Time For Absolutely No Reason, Even On Christmas Eve."

"It's a shepherd's pie," he said, but there was that telltale crook of his lips. "Mrs. Calloway's personal recipe, which she's made for me since I was a boy. It's good."

And if he looked faintly astonished by the fact he'd told her something that could have been construed as sentimental—almost as astonished as Zara felt—he covered it with that disgruntled expression of his. She sat down gingerly on the couch, automatically crossing her legs beneath her and wincing slightly as she felt a distant pulling sensation that reminded her what they'd been up to all evening.

"You're hurt," he accused at once.

Zara started to roll her eyes, but caught the look on his face. It was more than bad temper. It was much darker. Raw torment, she would have said, and a frozen look in those blue eyes of his that resembled winter now, chilly and bereft.

She made herself smile instead, then let it turn wicked. "Only in the best possible way."

He continued to stand there as she busied herself with the meal he'd brought. She took off the silver covers and helped herself to one of the plates. And a big gulp from one of the bottles of artisanal beer he'd brought along with them, dark and bitter and perfect. Nothing like socks at all. By the time she took her first bite, he'd moved away from the fire and sat down in the chair at the far end of the table. Jerkily. As if he'd thought better of it but was doing it anyway. Zara thought of wild animals then. Hurt and hungry and physically incapable, despite their own fierce needs, of coming closer.

"I had a kitten when I was little," she told him without daring to look at him. "She was my one true love and stayed strictly indoors. One day I came home from school to find a screen knocked out and the kitten gone. I searched everywhere. I sang into bushes and called her name up and down the street and into all our neighbor's properties. Ten days later, while I was calling for her one evening, I heard her reply."

"While I'm fascinated, of course, by tales of lost kittens and little girls," Chase said in a thin voice that was about as far from *fascinated* as it was possible to be without hurting them both on the sharp edge of all that sarcasm, "I think I told you not to tell me any more of your stories, Zara."

She slid a dark look his way. He looked elegant and dangerous at once, lounging back in the prissy armchair and owning it, somehow. Making it as riotously male as he was. His black hair looked as if he'd raked his fingers through it repeatedly. His laughably perfect chest was still on mouthwatering display, and he'd chosen to wear nothing but a pair of pajamalike bottoms in a black silk that hung very low on his narrow hips. He looked like a lazy, wanton, half-naked king, supernaturally impervious to the weather and that much more attractive because of it.

He made her mouth dry. She took another pull of her beer and ignored the narrow look he was giving her from those demanding blue eyes of his, that, despite his tone of voice, had warmed slightly since she'd started talking.

"She was under the hedge down near the woods on the edge of our lawn," Zara said, and smiled when he sighed. "I had to lie on my belly in the grass and talk to her, and after a while, she finally crept out. Inch by inch, but she wouldn't come all the way to me. Eventually I was able to reach out and grab her, and her heart...!" She shook her head, remembering the heat of the little body in her hand and the surge of protectiveness she'd felt then, filling her up to near choking. "It was *pounding*. So fast. So hard. Like she was terrified of the thing she wanted most."

Chase was ominously silent. Zara didn't look at him again. She applied herself to the hearty shepherd's pie before her, relishing every bite. Mrs. Calloway had outdone herself—and she was so hungry she even ate the peas slathered in gravy, when she normally avoided peas. For a while there was nothing but the sound of cutlery against china and the pop and rush of the fire in its grate.

And then Chase's voice, that dark rasp with all its precise British intonation that made her nearly squirm in her seat, cutting through all of that.

"Am I to take it, then, that I am the lost kitten in this scenario?"

Zara bit back her smile. "A much bigger one, of course. And fierce. Very fierce and mighty and male."

He watched her as if he was a very big cat, indeed.

"And what do you imagine it is I want most?" he asked quietly. "Yet am too terrified to claim?"

Zara picked up her beer bottle, more to hold it in her hands and disguise their tendency to shake than to drink it.

"I can't imagine," she said.

But she had imagined it, of course. She had too much imagination when it came to this man, and none of it was likely to help this situation any. It couldn't make her feel less fragile than she did just then, no matter how hard she fought to pretend otherwise. And it certainly couldn't compete with the reality of what had happened between them, all of which seemed to play on an endless, erotic loop in her head.

Maybe that was what gave her the courage to square her

shoulders and ask the thing she really wanted to ask him instead, because it mattered so much more now. So much more than she was prepared to admit, even to herself. And not because he'd told her she was beautiful—but because she'd been tempted to believe he meant it.

Zara met his gaze and held it. "Why don't you tell me the truth about why you went along with this ridiculous marriage?"

CHAPTER EIGHT

FOR A MOMENT, Chase thought he'd turned to ice at last.

That he'd finally frozen straight through, even as some part of him thrilled to the notion that she could read him that easily, that completely. That she could see so far into him she already knew what he had planned for New Year's Eve. His revenge. At last.

But she couldn't, of course. She might compare him to a lost kitten here in this warm room in the light of a flickering fire, but he wasn't one. The only thing he had in common with a pet cat were claws, and his, he was well aware, were by far the more damaging.

"I'm sorry," he said when she continued to look at him in that same expectant manner that made him want to tell her whatever it was she wanted to hear, simply to make her smile—a wholly alien notion that should have petrified him. "It's still the same reason it was before."

"And I'm sorry, too," she said, as unapologetically as he had, which might have made him smile had he not understood how serious this all was, whether he wanted it that way or not. She couldn't know. He shouldn't want her to know. Her knowing would help nothing, change nothing. "But I don't believe it."

"It's not a matter of belief," Chase said, very distinctly, in his CEO voice that allowed for no argument, only obedience. "It's a matter of fact. When I took over the company after my father died, no one was pleased. They'd read too many tabloids and paid too little attention to my actual achievements. Creditors who were content to take my father's word that they would be paid in due course felt no such allegiance to me, and called their markers. I needed an influx of cash, so I agreed to merge with Nicodemus Stathis, a union my father had always championed. But Nicodemus's agreement came at a price."

Zara's gaze moved over him then to the framed photographs above the fireplace. "Your sister."

Chase wondered what she saw. Her father had sold her off in much the same way, hadn't he? Was that what Chase was to her—a man so like her own father they were well-nigh indistinguishable? The very idea sickened him, but there was no denying the fact that this particular shoe fit all too well. Perhaps to beat Amos Elliott, he'd first had to become him. The notion stung.

"My sister, yes," Chase agreed, his lips twisting as he tasted the depth of how much he hated himself for that. He'd tried to protect Mattie his whole life and then he'd sold her off like a piece of furniture to the man she'd spent years running away from. *How proud their mother would have been of him*, he thought derisively. "And before you ask, no. She didn't want to marry him. I made her do it."

"I saw pictures of their wedding in the papers, like everyone else in the entire world," Zara said in that light way of hers that managed to wedge its way into him, forcing that brightness into all the places he wanted it least. *He hated it.* He wished he could hate her, too. It would make all of this so much easier—it would make it what he'd thought it would be when he'd concocted this revenge plan in the first place. It would make everything so much less complicated. "I failed to see a single shot of you standing over her with a gun to her head."

Chase eyed her, torn between ending this conversation

in a way likely to please him most as it involved his mouth on hers, or by simply getting up and leaving as he should. He had no idea why he did neither. Why he continued to sit there before her, as if those golden eyes kept him fastened to the chair.

Maybe they did more than that, because despite everything, he kept talking.

"The other pressing issue was that your father wanted me removed from my position altogether, and of course, he greatly influences how the board votes on such things," he said instead of any one of the things he could have said that might have been safer. "He insisted I join the happy Elliott family in exchange for his backing off on his campaign to have me removed as president and CEO of my own company." And then temper crept in, because why was he doing this? She wasn't a confidante. She was a chess piece. "We've already gone over this, haven't we? I was faintly drunk at our wedding. I didn't black out. I remember the conversation we had in the limo."

"Yes," she said after a too-long moment, and he couldn't read the expression on her face. "We've discussed parts of this before. But there are ways around my father, surely, that don't require marrying a stranger."

"Are there?" He raised his brows at her in stark disbelief that she, of all people, would say such a thing, and she flushed slightly. He had a predictable reaction to that, which he ignored. Or ordered himself to ignore, more accurately. "And yet here we both sit."

"I have Daddy issues, obviously," Zara countered in that rueful way of hers that was his undoing. Every time. "What's your excuse?"

Chase let out a laugh, however little humor it had in it.

"I suppose I have Daddy issues of my own," he admitted.

He couldn't look at her then. He thought that warm gaze

of hers must have some kind of sorcery to it, and it was making him say things he'd never, ever said to another living being. He glared at the fire instead, determined to resist her, and to keep himself from saying another word.

"That's nothing to be ashamed of, Chase." Her voice was warmer than the fire. Brighter. *Dangerous.* "I think you'll find that all children of powerful men have issues one way or another, even in the happiest and healthiest of families. It's the natural order of things."

"My father and I were never close," he was astounded to hear himself say, as if he was the kind of man who shared confidences. Who *talked* about things to the women he bedded. Or at all, to anyone. Ever. "I was a grave disappointment to him in all ways."

"How can that be?" she asked, and there was no judgment in her voice. Nothing knowing or insinuating, nothing sarcastic. She simply asked. "You're his successor. You worked in his company and your job wasn't all for show."

"You have no idea if it was or wasn't."

"In fact, I do." There was no malice in the way she said that despite his tone, just that quiet confidence of hers that he found more and more addictive each time he heard it. "I'm an excellent researcher, Chase. I know what your job was in London."

"Nonetheless, he felt my exploits were not a credit to the family name," Chase said stiffly, unwilling to dig any deeper into what she'd said, because it sounded like excuses. And lord knew he was filled to the brim with those, wasn't he?

He hadn't been a successor to his father in the way she meant. He'd been the cause of his father's worst nightmare. No amount of self-imposed exile in his mother's country or quiet competence in the family company was penance enough for his sins. He knew that too well. He'd been living it for the past twenty years.

"Exploits?" Zara asked him mildly. "That sounds exciting."

"It was too exciting for my father. My sister and I spent far too much time in the tabloids for his peace of mind," Chase said matter-of-factly. And then he kept going because why not? He'd already said too much. Why not compound the error? "He preferred Nicodemus to me. He said many times that Nicodemus was the son he wished he'd had instead."

He heard her shift in her seat and didn't want to hear whatever she might say next. He didn't want forgiveness. He didn't want absolution. He deserved neither.

"And I agreed with him, Zara. After he died, the only thing left was the company. I would do anything to save it." He looked at her then, and he knew it was a cold look. Harsh. Another warning she should heed—but she didn't flinch. Of course she didn't. Not Zara, who was afraid of being lifted but not in the least concerned by anyone else's demons. "I have. I will."

She stood then, surprising him. Then he told himself it was a good thing that she had the presence of mind to stop this train wreck of a conversation. He couldn't seem to walk away, so she would have to do it for the both of them—

Except Zara didn't storm off. She didn't move her gaze from his. She simply walked to him as if there was nothing more natural in the world. Then she threw a leg over him and sat herself down astride his lap, looping her arms around his neck as if they'd sat like this a thousand times before. As if she'd been made just for him.

As if they *fit*, key to lock. Perfectly crafted for each other, from head to toe.

He groaned, telling himself he was annoyed even as his hands moved to hold her there, pressed up against his sex so he could feel her softness. *Annoyed*, he reminded himself sharply as he moved to balance her better, to help her slide in and press those stunning breasts of hers closer to him.

"Tell me more about the things you have to do to save the company," she murmured, looking down at him in a way that made him burn much brighter than that piddling fire beside them. White-hot. Deep. "Did you have to sacrifice your body?"

"I did," he said, a low rasp, and she grinned. It was wicked and lovely, a promise that seared through him, making him hard and desperate for her that quickly. That completely. "It was terrible."

"You poor thing." She rolled her hips, making them both catch their breath, and then she laughed, throaty and low and designed to make him lose his mind. It would have worked, had he still possessed a mind to lose. "Why don't you tell me all about it?"

He tilted his head back and she angled hers down, until their lips were only the scantest breath apart and her hair swirled around them, cocooning them in the fragrance of it, red and sweet. As perfect as she was.

Mine, he thought. He felt it everywhere. Like a prophecy punched into his skin. *All mine.*

Zara smiled and shifted even closer. "I have all night."

Chase grinned back at her then. He forgot all the reasons he shouldn't succumb to this. Why he shouldn't allow the situation to get any worse than it already was. Why he shouldn't blur all these lines that much further than they already had, and when he knew where this was headed. Where it would have to end.

Instead, he took her at her word.

Zara walked out of the shower the next morning feeling very pleased with herself. With life in general, come to that. Certainly with the long, dark, wild night she'd had with Chase. So pleased, in fact, that she was humming a little "God Rest Ye Merry Gentlemen" as she toweled off, which was why it took her longer than it otherwise might have to hear the other melody that kept intruding on her admittedly off-key rendition of the happy carol.

Her cell phone, she realized when she heard the voice mail chime go off a moment later. She started toward the bedside table where she'd plugged it in, frowning when it started ringing again scant seconds later.

And that frown only deepened when she saw the name on her display.

Dad.

Zara swallowed. She sat down on the edge of the high bed, wrapping the towel tighter around her while everything she'd been feeling moments before spiraled out of her, as if off into a puddle on the floor at her feet.

But you are not a coward, Zara Elliott, she told herself briskly, *whatever else you might be, and Grams asked you to give him a chance, didn't she,* and then she picked the phone up and swiped the button to answer it before she could think better of it.

"Hi, Dad," she said chirpily. "Merry Christmas Eve!"

"Spare me the holiday nonsense, Zara," Amos said in his typically blunt, rude way. "Christmas is for feeble-minded idiots who need an excuse to spend money they don't have."

Nothing ever changed with her father. On some level, Zara supposed she ought to take a kind of comfort from that. She found she couldn't quite do it.

"That attitude is likely to get you put straight on the naughty list, mister!" she pointed out in the same too-cheerful voice—and then remembered that there were a thousand reasons not to talk to her father that way.

One of them being the thunderous silence that followed, during which she shut her eyes and covered them with her free hand, imagining Amos's gritted teeth and evil expression as if he was standing in front of her.

"I expected to hear from you by now," he said after a moment, and Zara understood that this was a gift. More of a gift than she'd received from her father in a long while. That he was ignoring her suicidal attempt to tease him and she should be grateful.

Except she didn't feel grateful.

Something new and much too hot charged through her, making her feel reckless and invulnerable at once.

"Has our relationship changed in some way?" she asked, and though she couldn't seem to control her mouth the way she knew she should, she used a mild, calm tone. As if polite defiance would go over better. "The last time I called home to chat you told me you'd let me know when you wanted to talk to me, and not to try to insert myself where I wasn't wanted. I believe that was my freshman year at Bryn Mawr."

There was a stunned sort of silence. Zara felt her heart beat too hard in her chest and told herself that was excitement. Victory, not fear.

"I don't think you want to test me," he growled at her, his tone even nastier than before. "Not when there's so much at stake."

"You called me, Dad," she pointed out, and she was sure she could actually hear her father gnashing his teeth. There was probably something wrong with her that she enjoyed it.

"We're having the usual Christmas dinner tomorrow at the house," Amos told her in that vicious way of his. "I expect to see both of you. You can leave the attitude behind. It's time to see if my investment is paying any dividends, and if I think you're in my way, I won't hesitate to crush you. I hope you're hearing me."

Zara heard him. But she chose not to focus on that part of what he'd said.

"And by 'your investment,' am I to assume you mean… me?" she asked drily. "Honestly, Dad, compliments like that are going to give me a big head. I might turn into Ariella before the end of the day if you keep that up."

"I mean the connection to the Elliott family, not you," Amos belted at her, loud and rough. She held her cell phone away from her ear and could still hear him perfectly. "And you better not be playing these dumb games of yours with Chase Whitaker. You better believe I would never have involved you in this if it could have been avoided—"

"You mean, if Ariella hadn't run away, proving herself perhaps slightly less trustworthy than the daughter who showed up and walked down the aisle?" Zara asked. "Maybe?"

It was like she had no control over her own bravado. It was easier over the phone, of course, where she wasn't within arm's reach—but this was bordering on insanity, surely. Or it was brilliant and long overdue, depending on how she chose to look at it.

And she knew exactly where the confidence to talk to her father like this had come from. *You are beautiful,* Chase had said, and it moved in her like courage. Now, when she needed it most.

"You need to do what you're told for once," Amos hissed then in that cold, horrible way that still got to her. Even when he wasn't in the same room. "Don't make me adjust that attitude for you. I don't think you'd like it."

Zara was sure she wouldn't. And then she despaired of herself. Because this man wasn't worth the loyalty she felt to him and she knew it, no matter what rose-colored glasses Grams might have worn. She kept thinking there was something she could do to make him say, *"Oh, my bad, of course you're wonderful—what have I been thinking all these years?"* When she knew very well there wasn't. He was worse than all the villains she studied, and scarier, because he was real. Hell, she had no naïveté left when it came to him, and she'd still married a stranger because he'd wanted it. Was it bold to throw some attitude his way—or sad that she still answered his phone calls?

"Are you listening to me?" Amos sounded even angrier, and something like incredulous. Because no one ignored him, did they?

"The thing is, Chase has his own set of Christmas traditions," Zara lied, pressing her fingers to her temple to ward off the headache this phone call was summoning. "It means a lot to him. There's no way he's going to abandon them for me. And in fact, pushing him might cause more harm than good." She heard her father mutter something and pushed on. "But he plans to attend the Whitaker Industries New Year's Eve party. I think he wants to start a new tradition. I assume you'll be there?"

"You have one week," Amos snarled at her. "I better not go to that party on New Year's and find out you've ruined something that I've spent a lot of time and energy working on. I promise you, you will not like what happens if I do."

And then he hung up. With a slam of the landline he still used into its cradle, making Zara's ears ring in protest.

"Merry Christmas to you, too," she muttered, and put her cell phone back down on the bedside table. Then she sighed, low and long and deep.

She didn't let herself dwell too much on her father, or the horrible way he both spoke to her and made her feel. She also didn't torture herself with worrying about what consequences he might heap on her for talking to him like that when she knew perfectly well that he wanted to hear nothing at all from her but quiet obedience, if that. What would be the point? Amos was Amos. The only question was why she kept putting herself in a position where he could say those hurtful things to her.

This was for you, Grams, she told her grandmother silently. *But this is the end of it.*

She walked over to the closet and went inside, dressing on autopilot. When she was done, she'd pulled on a pair of cream-colored velvet trousers and a dark green Henley top, as if her subconscious refused to let go of the holiday spirit no matter what a dampening influence Amos had been. She combed through her damp hair and tied it in a low knot at the nape of her neck. There was a full-length mirror in the dressing part of the walk-in closet, and she stared into it, not seeing all the ways her body and Chase's body had come together in the night, so miraculous and beautiful, but seeing her father's scorn instead. Hearing Ariella's lilting, malicious laughter. The music of her whole life.

This is a coup for you.

No matter how many times Chase had told her she was beautiful, or even set about proving it, she still saw what they did. An awkward woman, nothing like skinny, who would never be anyone's first choice for anything. It was the same thing she'd always seen.

The difference was, this time, it didn't make her sad. It made her furious. At her father, her sister. At herself. At this absurd situation she never should have let herself get trapped in no matter how great the temptation to be vindicated, to honor the one family member who had treated her well, *to prove herself at last—*

But the thought that she might have missed out on Chase, however temporary this was, however long it took her to recover from it when it was finished, made her heart ache inside her chest.

And she decided that made it as good a time as any to find out how her husband felt about the holidays.

She found him in the office high on the second floor in the wing of the house Mrs. Calloway had told her housed a selection of guest suites and a separate entrance, should business associates require access to the Whitakers yet not be suitable to mix with family.

Chase was frowning down at the laptop open before him, sitting at the great desk that loomed large in the center of the room with stacks of open files before him and several serious-looking binders filled with more documents at his elbow. The only noise in the room came from his fingers tapping against the keys, and Zara found herself caught there in the doorway, watching all that quiet ruthlessness of his turned to the details of the work a man in his position must have to do all the time, but which she'd somehow never imagined him doing. Smiting minions with a glare, yes. Typing out emails like mortal men? No.

She didn't move or even breathe hard, but he knew she was there almost at once. She saw him frown in the same instant his fingers paused on the keys, and then that wild blue gaze was slamming into her from across the room.

The last time she'd seen the blue of his eyes, it had been dawn enough that there was a faint shimmer of a matching color in the dark night beyond her windows and he'd been thrusting deep inside of her.

Zara felt heat rush over her, staining her cheeks and making her body shiver into total awareness. Chase allowed only that tiny crook of his clever lips. She still felt it like the sun bursting forth after a long afternoon of rain.

Oh, the dangers this man presented. She was already as good as lost.

"Do you celebrate Christmas?" she asked, because the only other thing she wanted to talk about might involve her launching herself over that great big desk to get to him, and what if he'd only intended that to be the one night it had been? She couldn't face it. "I'm assuming you must, given the amount of holiday decorations all over this house."

"The Calloways celebrate Christmas," Chase said, sitting back in his chair and threading his hands together behind his head. He wore the kind of long-sleeved shirt that looked simple and understated and which Zara knew was therefore exorbitantly expensive. It couldn't possibly cling to his every gorgeous muscle like that if it wasn't. "They take today and tomorrow off, of course. My father and Mattie used to have Christmas here. My father called that 'roughing it,' because my sister did the cooking."

Zara would not have imagined that someone like Mattie Whitaker knew her way around a kitchen, but that was the least interesting part of what he'd said. She leaned one shoulder against the door frame.

"Your father and Mattie? Not you?"

That hard, terrible thing she'd seen several times before moved over his face then. He sat forward and dropped his hands, then stood in the same smooth motion, as if whatever it was he was thinking of was too harsh to take while seated.

"Not me." He studied her for a moment. "I prefer to ignore Christmas." It looked as if he fought with himself then; she could see it flash in all that stark blue, and she didn't know if he lost or won, but he continued. "I have since my mother died."

She felt stricken. "You were only a kid when your mother died."

"Yes."

"And you never came here and joined in with your sister and father?"

A barely noticeable pause. "No."

Zara nodded. She told herself he couldn't possibly see that swell of sympathy for the boy he'd been flood through her.

"You're in luck then," she told him. "I've just declared this the anti-Christmas."

"We don't have to declare it anything," he said in that

harsh way of his that should have felt like a slap, but didn't. Maybe because she could see that dark thing in his gaze. Maybe because she mourned for a thirteen-year-old boy who had lost too much. "We can continue to pretend it isn't happening, which I've found has worked marvelously for the past twenty years."

"You'll be happy to know that I declined my father's generous invitation to spend Christmas at his house," she said as if he hadn't spoken. "You're welcome. I've been to that Christmas dinner many times, and let me assure you, it's not as much fun as it sounds. It's a bit more like the Inquisition. Everyone ends up drunk, in tears or both. I believe it's my father's favorite day of the year."

"Yet I bet you show up every single year anyway," Chase said, and not in a complimentary way. "Dutiful and obedient to the bitter end."

"The point," Zara said loftily, "is that I've spent a lot of time hiding in the guest bathroom in the far part of the house imagining what a perfect anti-Christmas would entail."

Chase moved from around the desk then, that predatory gleam in his gaze that sent Zara's heart into overdrive.

"If it doesn't feature you naked and in my bed, I'm not interested," he said, and then he was in front of her, sweeping her into his arms and picking her up again, making her head swim.

This time, she didn't fight with him. This time, she smiled.

"I think that can be arranged," Zara murmured, and then his mouth was on hers and she didn't care what day it was. She just wanted him again.

And again.

And again, like there was nothing in the world but this. But him.

Them.

For however long it lasted.

* * *

Chase hated Christmas. He preferred to spend the whole of it working, and had spent years telling himself that he enjoyed it that way. England had always seemed to more or less shut down from roughly the fifteenth of December onward, and he'd had a whole half month to himself. He could hide away from the world and no one questioned it, as they were all too busy adhering to their traditions and Christmassing themselves half to death.

But whatever Zara called what they were doing, he found he liked it.

They'd spent most of Christmas Eve in his bed, which had suited him fine. Chase had dedicated himself to truly memorizing every last one of her gorgeous curves, and then they'd slept wrapped around each other. In a manner that Chase was opting not to question or even look at too closely, as he doubted he'd like all the alarms that set off inside him.

And now it was late on Christmas morning, and Zara was standing in the kitchens of Greenleigh, wearing a pair of his boxers, that lush little cashmere thing she'd worn before and an adorable pair of thick socks. Her hair hung about in an untamed tangle of red that reminded him of all the times he'd wrapped it around his fists or buried his fingers in it throughout the night.

And she was cooking him pancakes, like every domestic daydream he'd ever had about a family life he'd always known he didn't deserve.

"Chocolate chip pancakes," she told him over her shoulder. "Because this is the one day a year that sugar doesn't count. Well, maybe the second day, depending on your feelings about Halloween."

He could fall in love with her, he thought then, watching her fondly from the far counter with a mug of strong, dark coffee at his lips—

And then froze. Appalled.

Because, of course, he already had.

He felt that rocket through him. He felt the ancestral stones buckle beneath his feet. He felt everything he knew to be true about himself quake, then shift.

He felt.

Not that Zara noticed.

"The ultimate Christmas morning delicacy is, obviously, cinnamon rolls, but I couldn't find the right ingredients," she was saying, completely unaware what had happened right there before her. Completely oblivious to the seismic event that had knocked him sideways. She glanced over at him and laughed. "What? Everyone has a pastry preference, Chase. It doesn't make you less of a man to admit it."

And Chase couldn't help himself. He surrendered.

She fed him hot, gooey pancakes, sitting cross-legged on the gleaming countertops. She made him laugh more in the course of a single morning that he thought he had in a year. In twenty years. She was like a fountain of joy, and he wanted nothing more than to bathe in it—and he did.

Despite what was coming. Despite what he knew he would do to her before this was over.

He laid her out over that same counter and he feasted on her. Their mouths met, sweet from the chocolate and still too hot to bear, and Chase stopped holding himself back. He stopped pretending he could.

He took her in the library, stretched out on the rug before the fire, then again in one of those leather chairs. He propped her hands against the windows that looked over the river and took her from behind, reveling in the things their bodies could do together. Reveling in all the things he felt with this woman that he'd never felt before—that he'd never imagined he *could* feel.

And when he wasn't sunk deep inside of her, when she

wasn't moaning out his name, she talked. She told him of her Gothic heroes and their naive maidens. She told him of her college friends and the adventures they'd had, far removed from the merciless glare of the public. She told him what it was like to work on her master's at Yale and how she'd meant to redecorate her grandmother's cottage once it had passed to her but had found she couldn't bear to change a thing.

She cast that spell of hers with every word, pulling him deeper with every story, until Chase couldn't help but believe. That he was a normal man. That this was like any other love affair and would simply bloom and grow the longer they were together.

He believed that he could keep from hurting her. He believed that he was the man she seemed to see when she looked at him in that way of hers, with her eyes so warm they rivaled the sun and that pretty smile on her mouth.

Chase wanted to be that man more than he could remember wanting anything.

He slept with her and he woke with her, and it was very nearly dizzying, how quickly he became accustomed to both. To the scent of her hair, the sweet smell of her skin. To the soft weight of her against him in the night. To the scratch in her voice when she woke, and the way she frowned at him until she had her coffee.

He let himself believe, even though he knew better.

And then, soon enough, reality intruded in the form of a curt phone call from his brother-in-law and new chief operating officer, and their time was up. And Chase knew that while he would never forget these days he'd spent with the woman who should never have become his wife, they might also be the death of him.

It felt like a fair trade.

"We leave for Manhattan today," he barked out at her over the breakfast they'd taken to having in the private salon off the master bedroom.

"Today?" she asked, reasonably startled.

"Today." He sounded like an ass and he couldn't seem to stop himself. It was that or throw away all of his plans and collapse into her—but he couldn't do that. This wasn't about him. It was about the company. It was about the debt he could never repay. It was about revenge. He scowled into his own coffee and saw nothing but the deep, clawing murk of the past. "As soon as possible. Mrs. Calloway is packing your things."

He felt the way she looked at him, reproachful and watchful at once, but he knew better than to look her way. He'd melt. Again. Possibly for good, and then he'd truly be the failure his father had gone to his death believing he was.

"Then we'd better not linger," Zara said in that way of hers that would have made him laugh the night before. That should have made him laugh now, but he could feel himself changing. Growing his once-impenetrable armor back even as he sat there across from her in the elegant little room.

Reverting to form, something whispered inside of him.

When he looked at her, he knew his face was blank, and he told himself he was just as hollow within. And it was as much a lie as all of this pretending had been. A lie or a wish—what difference did it make? He was still the man he was. The monster hiding in plain sight, with all of that blood on his hands.

"This has been a lovely holiday," he told her, his voice chilly. "But we've only two days between now and New Year's Eve and quite a bit to accomplish." When she only stared at him as if he'd grown a new head, he let impatience seep into his expression. His voice. "Do you have a problem with that?"

He watched her shift in her seat. Her legs were folded beneath her as always and she'd pulled on one of his button-down shirts, letting the silk caress those mouthwatering curves of hers in all the ways he wanted to do. She looked edible. She looked like *his*, damn it.

But her marvelous eyes were turning wary and that wicked, carnal mouth was pressed into a too-neutral line, and this thing that never should have started was finished. Chase knew it. He welcomed it. It was time to move on.

So there was no reason at all it should tear at him as it did.

"Certainly not," she said quietly, and the Zara he knew had disappeared again, behind that cool, competent shell he remembered from their first, early days. "I believe you tasked me with finding a dress that fits me. We'd best get moving. There's no telling how long a quest like that might take."

And he told himself to get used to it when she stood up and walked away from him, because this was only the beginning. Who cared if he mourned? He was good at mourning.

This was the easy part.

CHAPTER NINE

AFTER THE ISOLATION of Greenleigh, Manhattan was a dizzying rush. All of that speed and sound, the whirl of so many lights and that pulsing energy that settled deep in the bones. Gusts of arctic winds swept through the concrete canyons and temporarily blinded Zara every time she turned a corner, no matter how well she bundled herself up against the chill.

And it was the change of scenery that was making her feel off balance and strange, Zara assured herself, and not Chase's abrupt change of demeanor since he'd announced it was time to leave for the city.

You knew this wouldn't last, she reminded herself as she walked through the famed marble lobby of The Plaza hotel, a New York City landmark and one of Zara's favorite places on earth. The Plaza was where Grams had stayed whenever she visited the city while she was still alive, and Zara had a thousand fond memories of meeting her here for tea and spending nights on the roll-out bed in the well-appointed sitting rooms of the various suites she'd stayed in. *It's your own fault if you imagined it might.*

Her friends wanted updates about her feelings. The tabloids had found her email and harassed her daily for any and all hints of something scandalous they could run. Her father left increasingly angry voice mails. And Zara had ignored all of them and spent the past two days sitting in the study on the bottom floor of the two-story suite Chase had declared was theirs for the duration, ignoring the elegant, iconic French decor and dutifully working on her thesis. When she hadn't been making the rounds to the Manhattan dress shops she could tolerate—meaning, the ones her sister didn't patronize—to find a dress that Chase might think "fit her."

Which might very well have been his restrained, very British way of telling you that you looked fat at your wedding, she reminded herself.

Not that she disagreed. But she wished he'd never said that. She wished a lot of things. It was as if that brief spate of Christmas cheer had never happened. As if it was all nothing more than the fevered fantasies of the Ugly Duckling Elliott sister who'd stolen her sister's man, as the tabloids now told it.

Until he came to her late at night, that was.

In the dark, Chase was tormented and possessed, and he took her like their lives depended on it. Zara half believed that they might. The Manhattan lights kept their bedroom bright, but he was always in shadow, always moving over her and in her like those increasingly dark dreams of hers, never showing her all those parts of himself she'd thought she'd come to know well in that big old house of his upstate.

It didn't take a genius to understand that Chase was coming undone, and that it no doubt meant this marriage was, too.

Zara made her way to the elevator and stepped inside, telling herself to be philosophical. Resigned to the inevitable, not saddened by it. She'd known the risks when she'd introduced the physical into this bloodless marriage on paper. She'd known that what happened between them would never, ever be anything but temporary.

There is absolutely no use crying over spilled milk, she

told herself briskly as the elevator rose toward their floor. *There never is.*

No matter that she was desperately afraid that she might have fallen in love with him. That was her version of "casual."

Her version of casual sucked.

She let herself into the large, airy suite dotted with huge windows that overlooked Central Park and let in so much winter light it nearly burned. She shrugged out of her coat and kicked off her boots, padding on bare feet down the hall, past the study she'd set up as her office while Chase spent his time at the Whitaker Industries headquarters several blocks south, and into the living room with its great, gold-rimmed mirror arching high above the marble fireplace.

And then stopped in her tracks when she heard a very familiar peal of laughter wafting toward her down the staircase from the second floor.

From the bedroom.

Zara stood stock-still, not believing her own ears. This was her vast swath of insecurities talking, surely, treating her to an auditory hallucination—

But footsteps followed the laughter, and she watched in a frozen kind of horror as Ariella sauntered into view.

Her feet appeared first, clad in ankle boots with her typical skyscraper heels that made no concession whatsoever to the fact that it was late December and the city streets were icy and treacherous. Then her long, skinny legs, shown to great advantage in a pair of dark leggings that hugged every lean inch of them. Then her teeny-tiny hips, wrapped in some kind of complicated metal belt that made them look that much more slight and narrow. Then her much-photographed torso, shown to great advantage in a dark blazer with a gauzy scarf tossed around her neck.

And then she was *right there* on the stairs leading down

from the bed where Chase had kept Zara awake until well into the morning—only hours ago, Zara couldn't help but think—all that carefully highlighted blond hair gleaming in the afternoon light and a self-satisfied smirk on her face as she saw who waited for her below.

She took her time. Ariella had always enjoyed a good entrance.

"Just look at you, Pud," Ariella trilled, using that awful nickname that had once been *Pudding* that she'd bestowed upon Zara for eating too much dessert one miserable summer. "What have you been doing all day? Digging sewers in the outer boroughs?"

Until that moment, of course, Zara had believed she looked good. Better than good. She'd tamed her hair into a concoction featuring a number of braids and collected it all in a big bun that she'd thought looked pretty and interesting at once. She was wearing a royal-blue sweater dress that she'd imagined made all of her curves sing. She'd been looking forward to gauging Chase's reaction to it, though she'd told herself several lies about that, as that felt slightly pathetic and needy. Still. There it was.

And she hated the fact that one snide comment from her sister made her doubt what she'd seen with her own eyes in her mirror that morning and in the dress shop she'd just left after finally finding the perfect New Year's Eve gown.

But she merely smiled, because it had been a long time since she'd showed Ariella that kind of weakness.

"Did you get confused, Ariella?" she asked, infusing her voice with concern. "I know dates and times and responsibilities aren't your strong suit. You were supposed to turn up at the church in Connecticut over three weeks ago. Not here at The Plaza today."

Ariella came to the bottom of the stairs, stopped with a bit of dramatic license and rolled her eyes.

"He's not really your husband, Zara. You're not that

delusional, are you?" She laughed when Zara only stared back at her. "Or maybe you are. I don't know how to break this to you—" and she made sure to smirk again, then let her expression turn lascivious and pointed at once "—but *Chase* doesn't seem to think he's very married."

The twelve-year-old inside of Zara reacted exactly the way Ariella wanted her to react to that insinuation—with horror and upset. Far more of both than was warranted, she understood, from something she kept trying to tell herself was "casual." But the rest of Zara was much older than twelve and had been dealing with Ariella for far too long to take anything she said to heart.

That Zara sighed. "Let me guess. You really don't like the fact that the tabloids are suggesting that I could steal a man from you."

"Because you couldn't!" Ariella spat at once. "The very idea is hilarious! *Look* at you!"

And then she waved her hand up and down, taking Zara in with the loopy gesture, making Zara feel tiny and hugely fat at once. As intended.

Zara locked that away. This wasn't junior high school, no matter how her sister behaved.

"Let this be a lesson to you, Ariella," Zara said very calmly. "When you run away from your own arranged wedding ceremony, someone else might be called upon to take your place. And the tabloids might draw their own conclusions."

Ariella glared at her, her hazel eyes narrowing. "You're loving this, aren't you?" she asked softly. "You've waited your whole, sad life for this kind of attention."

It was Zara's turn to roll her eyes. "Oh, yes," she said. "I love each and every demonstration of how little you think of me. It warms my heart. And it's always been my dearest wish to be neck-deep in one of Dad's ugly little plots. This is all a dream come true."

Ariella pursed her lips, then sashayed over to the long, ornate couch, sweeping up the long, black coat Zara had failed to notice was tucked away on the far side.

"Enjoy it while you can," Ariella advised coolly. Then she looked up, as if she could see past the gleaming chandelier and into the master bedroom suite above them, and smiled that smug smile of hers again. "I know I did."

Zara observed, as if from a far greater distance than simply the length of the sitting room bathed in too much sharp December light, that despite all the thousands of ways her sister had insulted and hurt her over the years, this was the first time she thought she really might haul off and punch her. Preferably right in her face.

But she knew better than to say anything—to give Ariella any more ammunition or satisfaction, especially if it could be construed as jealousy over Chase. She only crossed her arms over her front and waited as her sister took her sweet time buttoning up her coat and then pulling on her sleek leather gloves.

"I'll be sure to tell Dad that things are *finally* in check," Ariella was saying, sounding delighted with herself. "I know he'll be relieved. And I suppose I'll see you at the New Year's Eve party. If you still insist on coming."

"Chase wants me there," Zara replied, though she knew better than to engage like that. There was no winning a fight with someone who wasn't fighting for anything— whose single goal was to inflict pain. No winning and no point trying. But she couldn't seem to help herself. "And I am nothing if not a dutiful wife, Ariella. I find I've taken to the role like it was made for me."

Ariella didn't like that, Zara could see, and that just about made this whole scene worth it. Her pretty face twisted in something like disgust. Or maybe it was pure rage.

"It wasn't," Ariella said, and her voice was poisonous. "Like everything else, it was made for me, and you're the unwanted, unattractive backup plan. Too bad, Pud. But then, you can't imagine this was ever going to work out, can you?"

Her derisive laughter told Zara what she thought of that. And then she flounced toward the door, her ridiculous heels loud in the long hallway. Zara trailed after her automatically, leaving enough distance between them that she might—*might*—fight off the urge toward violence.

"I don't need an escort to find my way out," Ariella said as she opened the door and looked back over her shoulder. "I didn't need one on my way in, either."

"Don't be silly, Ariella," Zara replied, summoning up another smile, though this one was much sharper than its predecessors. "I'm making sure the door is locked. This is New York City. You never know what garbage might roll in off the streets."

Ariella looked surprised for a moment, but then she laughed in her superior way and closed the door behind her. And she was gone, leaving nothing but the faint scent of her perfume—a lovely bit of something citrus, of course, everything about her was calculated to be effortlessly lovely—behind.

Zara's hands shook as she threw the dead bolt, and she imagined that she could hear further peals of laughter from the hall beyond. Ringing in her ears. Taunting her. She gritted her teeth and turned back to the suite, glaring ferociously at the floor and her own feet in the tights she'd worn against the bitter cold outside. She ordered herself not to think about it. Not to give Ariella what she wanted. Not to succumb to that same self-hating madness that had chased her across so many years.

It didn't matter what Ariella had been doing here. It didn't matter what might or might not have happened between her and Chase. Because she might have the title at the moment, but Zara wasn't really his wife. She knew that. She *knew* it—even if her heart balked.

He was never yours, a caustic voice told her, harsh and true. *You can't lose something you never had to begin with.*

But when she walked into the living room, Chase was standing on the stairs that led up to the second story, staring down at her with a black look on his face and his wild blue eyes like a hard slap.

"Why the hell do you let her speak to you like that?" Chase demanded, incredulous, when that wasn't what he'd meant to say at all.

Zara stiffened, pulling herself up to her full height in the arched doorway to the hall and the door beyond, looking like a bloody queen in a soft dress that licked all over her the way he couldn't seem to stop yearning to do. The way that was driving him mad even now, when he entertained the foolish notion that he might protect her.

He, who would only hurt her, and well did he know it. It was laughable. But still, it worked in him, like need. Like madness.

"If there is a way to stop Ariella doing exactly what she wants, when she wants to do it, I've never discovered it," she said in a light, airy voice he didn't believe at all. "Did you fare any better?"

Chase scowled at her. "Is that an accusation?"

He watched her hands ball into fists and something very old and very tired moved over her face. It made that foolish thing in him that wanted so desperately to play the hero for her shift to full alert. It made him wish her sister were a man so Chase could have dealt with her as she deserved.

"We might be married," Zara said, her voice bland and cool and *he hated it,* "but I'd have to be a particular brand of idiot to imagine those vows meant anything to you. You're not required to keep any promises to me." Her gaze was dark and it hit at him. Hard. "Nevertheless, I'd like to think you're not stupid enough to sleep with Ariella when she's that obviously playing one of her games. No doubt at my father's urging." She shrugged. "But then again, the male libido makes its own rules, doesn't it? Or so says the history of the world."

Chase felt a muscle in his jaw tense, and he didn't know if he walked down the remaining stairs toward her to protect her—or make her pay, somehow, for thinking less of him when he knew that was what he should want. When it was no less than he deserved.

He should let her think he'd done exactly what Ariella wanted her to think he'd done. It would make everything easier.

"Of course I didn't touch her," he said instead, and there was no reason for it. Only Zara's lifted chin, her challenging gaze. Only that perfect mouth of hers and that stillness in the way she held herself that made him want to hold her instead. "She was here all of three minutes before you arrived, she was decidedly not welcome and I made no secret of that, and I've no idea how she wrangled a key from the front desk."

"Really?" Zara's voice was bone-dry. "No idea at all?"

He ignored that because there was a bleakness in her face then, and he couldn't stand it.

"Does she always speak to you in that manner?" he asked.

There was something he didn't understand in that hard gleam in her eyes, some truth he couldn't decode in the way she pressed her lips together, and she didn't answer him. She stalked deeper into the sitting room instead and didn't stop moving until she stood at one of the long windows.

"I'll take it that she does," he said to the fine line of her too-straight back. He wanted too many things that didn't make sense. To set her free, now, before he hurt her the way he thought he would. To gather her close and never let her go. To defend her. To help her. To change all of this before it swallowed them both whole. To believe that somehow, it wasn't already too late. "Zara, I don't want—"

"I suppose your family is perfect then," she said, and she sounded much farther away than she was, as if she'd catapulted herself out into all that winter sunshine and hung somewhere over the chilly expanse of Central Park. As if she was already gone. As if he'd already done the thing that would make her leave. His revenge. "No tensions, no arguments. No underlying darkness informing even the most banal of interactions. Just endless years of bliss and harmony. You're very lucky, Chase. But not everyone can say the same."

He didn't know what that was, that terrible thing that shook through him, an earthquake of devastation and determination, and it had too much to do with that bleak note in her voice. And that deep, black hurt where his heart should have died twenty years ago. Until Zara, he'd thought it had.

"I killed my mother."

Chase didn't know where that had come from.

For a stunned, breathless moment he thought he hadn't truly said such a thing, hadn't thrown it out like that, bald and ugly in the midst of this delicate, pretty room—that it was only inside his head, where it belonged, where it needed to stay locked up in the dark—

But Zara turned, slowly.

He didn't know what he expected to see on her face. Shock? Horror? Disgust?

She only held his gaze and waited.

And he hadn't wanted to blurt that out in the first place. He didn't know why he had. He wanted to turn and leave. To disappear into the cold embrace of this careless city and never return to this place, this subject, this woman with golden eyes who saw too much.

Instead, he moved a step closer.

"We were on holiday in South Africa. We'd been meaning to take a family trip that day, but my father was called away on some business thing or another, so it was only the rest of us." He bit out the words like they might fight back if he didn't, staccato and stern. As black as his soul. "Mattie and I were in the back. She was only little, and she kept singing this annoying song over and over. She wouldn't stop. I was cruel to her, of course, because I was thirteen and I knew there was nothing she hated so much as being called a baby."

He searched her face, but there was nothing. No reaction, no accusation. Just Zara, waiting. As if there was nothing he could say that was terrible enough to make her look at him any differently than she did then.

And he *wanted* her to know the truth, suddenly. He wanted her to see exactly who he was, so she'd stop looking at him like that. Like she had at Greenleigh, as if he was someone so much better than he was. Someone washed clean. Someone untainted by the things he'd done.

Someone worthy of her, the way he'd pretended he was for those too-few days.

"There was a man in the road," he said, his voice scratchy. After all these years, he remembered it so well. In such perfect, damning detail. "I teased Mattie about that stupid song until she hit me. My mother turned around—I remember her laughing—and then I saw the man standing there in our lane at the same time the driver did."

He shook his head, and Zara shifted, but only to fold her arms over her front in that way she had that made him envision her as the professor she'd told him she wanted to become one day, in the future when this odd little interlude of theirs was nothing but a dim, dark memory for her.

When she was free of this. Of him.

But at least she'd know exactly who it was she'd been

shackled to for so short a time. He could give her that gift. It could only help her forget him that much faster.

"There was a loud noise, like the tire going out," he said, and he realized as he did that he'd never said any of this out loud before. He'd never told this story. He'd never imagined he would want to tell it to anyone. "The driver swerved and didn't move again. He was shot, though I wouldn't know that until afterward."

Until Big Bart had told him the barest facts and instructed him to say nothing. Ever. To pretend it was an accident, for all their sakes.

"Oh, Chase," Zara breathed.

"When the car finally skidded to a stop, we'd tumbled all around. I ended up on top of Mattie. My mother was bleeding, and that was before they dragged her from the car." He was seeing more past than present then, but he saw the way her arms moved, her hands rising to cover her mouth, her eyes wide and dark with pain. "She looked right at me. She saw me. She was terrified." He swallowed, hard. "And then she told the men who held her that they'd killed her children, that her children were dead—and I covered Mattie's mouth with my hand and I held her down, so she couldn't see anything. I played dead." He stared at Zara, he mourned her, and then he said it. He spat it out, the words like poison. "And I did absolutely nothing when those men beat my mother before my eyes. Or when they shot her, too."

The room felt heavier then. Diseased, just as he was. As he must always have been, to do such a thing.

Zara didn't say anything for a long moment, and when she finally moved her hands from her mouth, all Chase could see was that too-bright warmth in her eyes. The same as always. Brighter, perhaps. He didn't understand it.

"How are you here?" she asked, her voice too quiet. "How did you survive?"

He didn't understand that question, either. "There was a passing lorry. The driver stopped and scared them off." He scowled at her. "That's all that you have to say? I did nothing. I was right there and *I did nothing.*" He laughed, and even he could hear it was an awful, broken sound. "It's what I do."

"What should you have done?" she asked. There was no accusation there. No horror. It sounded like a simple question and it tore at him.

"I should have done what anyone would have done!" he raged at her. "I should have helped her!"

"How?"

She asked it so calmly. So easily. Chase felt his heart pound in his chest. Too hard. Too fast. He felt as if something giant and merciless had him fast in its grip and was tightening its hold. He felt suspended over a great abyss he couldn't even name. And all she did was stare back at him, her golden gaze so warm it made him feel scraped raw.

"Should you have abandoned your sister? What if she'd sat up and seen what was happening? What would those men have done to her?" Her voice was so calm, so cool, and Chase was sure that somehow, despite that, it was hacking him into pieces. He felt paralyzed. He felt inside out. And she only kept going. "Or perhaps you could have run out of that car and had those men beat you and shoot you in front of your mother first. Would that have been better?"

"You don't understand." He barely recognized his own voice, and he had no memory of moving, of closing the distance between them, but she was still before the windows and then he was, too. "You weren't there."

"No," she agreed. "But what you're describing—"

"I killed her as surely as if I shot her myself."

He didn't recognize his own voice, only the raw thing that the words left behind where his throat had been.

"Your mother wanted to save you, Chase," Zara said softly. Carefully, he thought, though her eyes were still so bright. "That's why she told those men you and Mattie were already dead, don't you think? Would you really undo her last sacrifice if you could?"

If the walls had started crumbling around them then, Chase wouldn't have been at all surprised. *He* was crumbling, collapsing, toppling into ash and dust, and the only thing he was sure of was that *she* was at the center of it. He wrapped his hands around her shoulders and pulled her closer, feeling outside his skin. Utterly destroyed.

"Don't you dare," he seethed at her. More monster in that moment than he'd ever been man. "Don't you dare forgive me."

Her lovely face crumpled in on itself, which he felt like a kick to his side, and then she smoothed it out somehow and offered him that smile of hers. *That* was like a kick to the head.

"Because you can't forgive yourself?" she asked. She reached up and took his face between her hands, as if he was only a man, after all. A broken, solitary man who couldn't possibly deserve all that light that beamed at him from her gaze. "Chase, you must know you couldn't have saved her. You were *thirteen*. There was only one of you, and someone had to take care of your sister."

Chase felt torn in two. He shook his head, breathing as hard as if he was running flat out through the streets of Manhattan. As if he was fighting off those ghosts that had haunted him for twenty years with his own fists, the way he'd dreamed he'd done. The way he wished he'd done.

"It doesn't matter how hard you train or how diligently you punish yourself or how completely you isolate yourself from the world," she told him, her voice so serious, her eyes so wide, tears he was stunned to understand were *for him* making gleaming tracks down her cheeks. "You can't change the fact that you're not the villain, Chase. You were a victim, too."

And he channeled all of those things inside of him, all that darkness, all those howling storms, into that dangerous heat that still moved in him—that always moved in him when she was near.

He couldn't answer her. He didn't know how. So he kissed her.

And he poured it all out. His anguish. His grief. The long years of hating himself, the separation from his family. All the things he'd called the monster in him. All the ways he'd made himself pay.

He poured it all into her, and she took it.

She took it and she reveled in it. When he went to strip that dress from her perfect body, she helped him. When he picked her up and walked her backward until she was up against the wall, she wrapped her legs around his hips and sank down onto him, sheathing him deep inside of her.

Like she was fluent in any language he might try to speak to her.

He put one hand flat against the wall, kept the other at her bottom to support her, and then he rode them both hard and wild and screaming into oblivion.

And it wasn't enough.

Nothing will ever be enough, something that felt like truth, like fate, whispered inside of him.

He was like a man possessed. He carried her up to the master bedroom and he took his time, licking his way across every inch of her lovely, flushed skin like that might bring any remaining secrets between them to the surface. Like that might heal them both.

Maybe it would, he thought. *Maybe it truly could.*

He lavished her with all the love and need and hope he'd carried around for too long, locked away so deep within him even he hadn't realized it was there.

"You're not to blame," Zara told him again and again, until it was like poetry.

He couldn't say he believed that, but he heard her. And the more she said it, the more those dark things in him yielded before the onslaught of all that glorious light.

Before *her*.

He ordered food at some point from the butler service that came with the suite and he fed her himself, like she was the queen he'd often imagined her. He took her into the spacious bath and soaked them both, muttering words he knew he'd regret later, but couldn't seem to stop from simply coming out of him, like she'd opened something up in him he'd never fully close again.

"I love you," he told her, fierce and foolish, while her tears still fell and mingled with the water all around them, like some kind of baptism he didn't deserve. "And you'll regret that, too. Trust me, Zara. You will wish you never met me, and you will curse the day you tried to heal me. The only thing that happens to the people I love is—"

"Chase," she said, twisting around in the bath and pulling his mouth down to hers. "Shut up."

He lost himself in her. He found himself in her.

And when he woke the next morning, she was draped over him as if she'd been expertly handcrafted to fit him *just so*. He brushed a hank of her fiery hair back from her face and almost smiled at the cranky little noise she made before burrowing into his chest, refusing to open her eyes.

He had never felt anything like this—a great wave of something too intense to name that swept over him, through him, into him. Nothing had ever felt like this before, in as long as Chase could remember. Nothing had ever been so *right*.

But it was New Year's Eve. Their time was up. Before

the clock struck midnight, no matter what happened with the company, he would lose her forever.

He knew he would. It was just as he'd planned from the start.

CHAPTER TEN

"IF YOU'LL COME this way." The deferential young man who Zara knew was Chase's assistant politely indicated that she should follow him through the throngs of luxuriously dressed New Year's revelers, all of whom crowded into the Whitaker Industries ballroom high above Manhattan in their upper-class, expensive splendor. "Mr. Whitaker is gathering the board for a quick word before the ball drops."

"I'm not on the board," Zara said—stupidly. This man would know that already.

But she couldn't seem to help herself or the chill that rolled through her. Her hand clutched too hard around the stem of her wineglass, and she thought for a wild moment that she might snap it off. Then drop the whole mess of it on her own feet. Wouldn't *that* be elegant? Ariella—whose malevolence Zara was certain she could scent in the air, like incense—would love it.

Chase's assistant smiled. "Your presence was specifically requested."

Zara wanted to bolt. That was her first panicked reaction, and it ran deep, so deep that she shivered slightly and curled her toes hard into the too-high sandals she should have known better than to wear tonight. She wanted to leave this sparkling party, filled to the brim with so many fake smiles to her face and whispers behind her back, and run until everyone forgot, once again, that Ariella Elliott had a younger sister at all, much less that Chase Whitaker had married her.

It was the sandals that decided her. They were made for sauntering about like a woman with great confidence, not running away from the inevitable. She'd be more likely to trip and fall than make it out of this place, and she thought the humiliation of such a thing might actually kill her.

Pull yourself together, she ordered herself sternly.

"Of course," she said to Chase's assistant, and smiled coolly. "Lead the way."

And then she picked up the long, flowing skirt of her dress and followed him. He led her out of the warm, brightly lit ballroom and down one of the gilt-edged, dark-wood-accented hallways that proclaimed the Whitaker wealth and status in unmistakable terms. It was quieter here, away from the crowd and the band and the anticipation of midnight. It made it impossible for Zara to be anything but all too aware that in every way that mattered, she was marching toward her own execution.

Which, funnily enough, made her think of a very similar forced march she'd made almost a month ago now, down the aisle in her hometown church.

At least this time, the damned dress fits, she told herself balefully, running her free hand over her hip and letting the smooth, pretty material soothe her.

It had been a very long day. Elastic and interminable.

Chase had been gone before she woke up, much later in the morning than she was used to waking, after such a torrid night. He'd left her instructions to meet him at his office that evening, and she'd had nothing to do but sit in that hotel suite and stew over…everything. By the time her dress had been delivered in the afternoon, she was in a state even the longest bath imaginable couldn't soothe. Yet somehow, despite her gnawing certainty that something terrible was about to happen, was *already* happening, the night had eventually fallen. The hours had finally passed.

And soon enough she'd found herself walking into Chase's vast, sleek CEO's domain in the corner of the top floor in the Whitaker Industries offices, and all of that waiting had felt like no more than an instant.

He was so beautiful, she'd thought, as stunned as if she was seeing him for the first time. Men like him were the reason formal wear had been invented, and the tuxedo he'd worn with such nonchalance made him look nothing short of edible, perfectly highlighting his lean, athletic form. His black hair had been a touch too long, his dark blue eyes had still been the color of lost things and winter seas, and she'd known then, what that mouth felt like when he whispered that he loved her, again and again, until her skin felt tattooed with it.

She'd felt marked. Claimed and entirely his—no matter that deep down, she'd known better.

"Have I mentioned that you're beautiful?" Chase had asked gruffly, his mouth a stern line and only the faintest gleam in that stunning blue gaze of his as he looked down at her. "Particularly tonight." His gaze had dropped, then heated to a hungry wildfire as he'd taken in what she was wearing. "Particularly in that dress."

"Well," she'd said mildly, "it fits."

It did more than fit. It was a marvel, and Zara had known it the moment she'd finally found it. The dress was a deep burgundy with contrasting red panels at the sides, flowing down from studded cap sleeves to the floor in a gauzy fall of fabric that hinted at her legs beneath. It sported a deep V in front that plunged down between her breasts almost to her navel, before being caught in a belt that cinched in at her waist and showed off her figure in a vaguely Grecian fashion. And that was the dress's true beauty: when she wore it, even when she'd tried it on in a tiny dressing room all by herself in a boutique on Madison Avenue, Zara felt the way she did when Chase looked at her.

It was a miracle in red. It made her feel like one herself.

He'd looked at her then for a long, heart-stopping moment, like he had nothing else to do for the rest of his life but that.

"Yes," he'd said, his voice that low rasp that had made her body prickle with heat, her core melt, her skin flush. "It certainly fits."

There hadn't been time for the need she'd seen in his gaze then, the white-hot surge of desire that had made her tremble when he'd taken her hand. He'd only offered her his arm and walked with her the way he had once before on that cold, Connecticut morning, only this time, he hadn't seemed at all drunk. Or furious.

If she'd allowed herself to think about it, she'd have said he seemed…as broken as he did determined, despite all the ground she'd foolishly thought they'd covered the night before.

I love you, he'd told her, again and again. The way he'd told her she was beautiful. And she was almost tempted to believe him, the way she had then.

But there had been no time for that, either. There had been Whitaker Industries employees and clients to meet as Chase's wife rather than Amos's problematic daughter. Speculation in all of those eyes she'd pretended not to notice, whispers everywhere she walked she'd pretended not to hear.

Even Chase's intimidatingly gorgeous sister, Mattie, who didn't look at all unhappily married to the ferocious-looking man who stood beside her, holding her waist in a protective, possessive manner.

"I can't believe Chase didn't invite us to your wedding," Mattie had said with a polite smile that Zara hadn't quite believed, though she'd dutifully returned it. "But then, the finer points of wedding etiquette seem to escape my brother, as I'm sure you've noticed."

"A Whitaker family trait," the alarmingly intense Nicodemus Stathis had said silkily from beside her, which had made Mattie's smile slip into something far more intimate.

More to the point, it had saved Zara having to reply. And Chase had muttered his excuses and moved them along to the next group of people they had to meet and greet.

"She doesn't know what happened that day," he'd rasped, his hand tightening on her back as they'd moved away. Zara's heart had seemed to contract in her chest. "My father wanted her to think it was an accident."

"Someday," Zara had said quietly, "you're going to have to tell her the truth."

He'd slid a dark look her way. "I can't imagine why."

She'd frowned at him. "Because it's her story, too," she'd said. "You shouldn't have to carry the weight of it by yourself, and she shouldn't have to stay out in the dark. It's not fair to either one of you."

"I can handle it," he'd muttered.

"Chase." She'd frowned at him, then remembered where they were and had forced her expression back to neutral. "You have a sister who would love you, I bet, if you let her. Not everyone can say that." And she'd finally admitted the truth that had surely been obvious to the entire world, but which she'd steadfastly refused to acknowledge her whole life. "I can't."

Chase had looked startled. Then something much darker. And there'd been no time for him to respond as she'd been certain he'd wanted to do, because there'd been this business associate, that connection. The business of his position, which meant hers, too.

"It's through here," Chase's assistant said then, opening

a door and reaching out to take her glass from her. She surrendered it a beat slower than she should have. "See that archway? The board room is just inside."

Zara murmured her thanks and walked on, feeling that cold panic again, starting from that knot in her stomach and radiating outward, because she already knew what was going to happen here, didn't she? Maybe not the particulars, but she'd known since she'd woken up alone this morning that this was all a goodbye. A long, painful, darkly passionate goodbye.

A long time ago they'd talked about ammunition. Target practice. *War.* How silly of her to think that what had followed rendered all of that moot. How terribly, inexcusably foolish.

It wasn't a surprise then, when she stepped into the magnificent glass-and-steel boardroom to find her father and sister talking quietly at one end of the long table. They fell silent as she walked inside, wearing identical frowns.

Wonderful, Zara thought, and ordered herself to smile. Even though it hurt.

Especially because it hurt.

She recognized most of the men arrayed around the table, all of them businessmen like her father, corporate and ruthless and sleek, no matter how merry the smiles they aimed her way. Not that it stopped her returning them, as if she was wholly at her ease.

And at the other end of the table stood Chase, with Nicodemus at his side. Mattie sat in one of the chairs that lined the far wall, an enigmatic curve to her mouth and her gaze on Zara.

"Excellent," Chase said, and she heard too much foreboding in his dark voice. Too much triumph and all that must mean. "Now we can start."

"Take a seat, Zara," her father barked at her.

But it all felt too fraught with peril. Too portentous and

strange, so Zara shook her head and folded her arms across her waist, leaning nonchalantly against the great arch.

"I'm fine right here," she demurred.

"Let's talk about you, Amos," Chase suggested in a voice she'd never heard him use before. His dark blue gaze touched hers, and it was like a flare of wild blue agony. Then he turned it on her father. "I was planning to make this the cornerstone of my speech at midnight in front of all our guests and esteemed members of the press, but out of respect for your daughter, I decided to make this more private."

"What the hell are you talking about?" Amos growled in that way that still made hairs rise on the back of Zara's neck.

"I'm talking about malfeasance," Chase said with cold precision. And no apparent attempt to disguise his own satisfaction. "A case could even be made for moral turpitude. I'm calling a vote to have you removed as chairman of this board, Amos."

"This is pathetic," Amos sneered as the other board members shifted and started murmuring to each other. "Do you really think this kind of childish attack will do anything but show us all how ill suited you are for your position? Your father must be spinning in his grave."

Beside Chase, Nicodemus shifted, thrusting his hands in the pockets of his trousers. Zara thought he looked like nothing so much as a bodyguard just then—a furious and capable bodyguard, whose attention was focused solely on her father.

"Those are serious accusations, Chase," Nicodemus said then, his rough, faintly accented voice cutting through the rising clamor in the room. "I assume you do not make them lightly."

Amos started to snarl something else, but Chase's voice overrode his, that cool, precise voice of his impossible not to heed.

"I do not," he said.

Then he turned, and it took Zara a dizzying, world-tilting moment to realize that he was looking straight at her. And then in a moment, so was everyone else.

"Zara," Chase said quietly, "why did you marry me?"

For a moment she couldn't speak. Too many things were tearing through her head, then falling like stones through the rest of her. *Ammunition*, she thought. It had always been heading here. Straight here. At last, she understood.

"Tell the truth, Zara," her father advised her in his usual, nasty way. It made her shudder.

But it was Chase she couldn't look away from. Chase, who had said he loved her. Chase, who had called her beautiful. Chase, who she'd known better than to believe. It wasn't until this very moment that she understood how deeply she'd wanted it all to be real.

Or how much she loved this man she knew, now, she really and truly could never have. Because he'd always been going to betray her exactly like this. There was no way this hadn't been his plan all along. It had all been about her father and this company, never about her.

This really had been target practice.

Her father shifted in his chair, managing to transmit his usual aggression from across the long room. Chase only stared back at her, all that wild blue unreadable. And Zara felt frozen in place. As if, were she able to draw this moment out as long as possible, if she could simply stop time right here and now, all the things she'd wanted to believe before she'd walked into this room could still be true.

"Way to draw out the suspense, Pud," she heard her sister say then, acerbic and amused. *Smug*.

And something inside of Zara simply broke. One moment it was there, and then it was gone, and she felt all the things in her that had frozen come back to life that quickly. Like the flip of a switch.

I'm sorry, Grams, she thought in that instant. *I tried.*

"I married you because my father made me marry you," she said, and she was surprised to hear how strong and smooth she sounded. As if she was either of those things. She tilted her chin up and pressed on, ignoring everything but that heartbreak of blue that gazed back at her. "He demanded that you marry his daughter so he could control you. And by extension, this company."

"And if I didn't?" Chase asked softly.

"He would remove you as CEO and president." She smiled faintly at her father's bellow of outrage. "He was quite clear about the consequences. I believe he said he would crush you either way."

"So help me, Zara—" Amos growled.

"I should say that, of course, I wasn't the first choice. He meant for you to marry Ariella. She makes for a much better conspirator. I'm really only any good with books."

Amos shot to his feet.

"This is nothing but lies," he snapped. "The two of them cooked this up. It's all a calculated maneuver to oust me—"

"You are ousted either way, old man," Nicodemus told him. "Between us, Chase and I now control seventy percent of this company. How do you think that will end for you, no matter what happens here tonight?"

"And why would I tell a lie that makes me look this pitiful?" Zara interjected then, tearing her gaze from Chase's and frowning at her father, wishing she felt as if she was seeing him for the first time—but no. He was the same man he'd always been. She simply wasn't the same woman. She had Chase to thank for that. "You've never treated me with anything but contempt, yet I married a complete stranger because you ordered to do it. Because I had some fantasy that I could prove I was a good daughter. When the truth is, there is absolutely nothing I could ever do to please you. It took a forced march up an aisle and a

monthlong marriage to a man you promised to my sister
first, but I get it, Dad. I finally get it." She shifted, then
looked back at Chase. For the last time, she thought, and
so what if that tore her apart. She would survive that, too.
Eventually. "Believe me, I get it."

And then she turned with all the dignity she could manage, whatever shreds of grace she'd ever had at her dis-
posal, and kept her head held high as she walked away.

No matter that she left her heart there behind her, in
pieces on the boardroom floor.

Chase caught up to her as she cut through the ballroom,
the fastest way to the elevators.

He'd left the shouting to Nicodemus, knowing his
brother-in-law was more than capable of handling the
angry crowd and the necessary vote. By the end of the
night—before midnight, if he had to guess—it would all
be over. Chase would take his rightful place as chairman of
the board and CEO. Nicodemus would become president as
well as COO. And together they would usher Whitaker Industries into its next phase, as Big Bart would have wanted.

And Chase didn't care. His heart hurt, and he felt empty,
and that didn't change when he took her by her arm and
turned her around to face him. Because her eyes were all
shadow and darkness, and he thought it might cut him in
two.

"How can there possibly be anything more to say?"
she asked, and she didn't sound like herself. She didn't
sound like *Zara*. Her voice was brittle and harsh, as cold
as her gaze. "Will you deny me three more times before
the crowd sings 'Auld Lang Syne'? How biblical. Perhaps
I should stone myself while we're at it, for a truly prehis-
toric feel—"

"Stop," he rasped, and there were too many people
around. Too many avid gazes trained right on them, and

he wasn't sure she'd go with him if he tried to move this conversation somewhere private. In fact, he knew she wouldn't.

He did the next best thing. He swept her into his arms and out into the middle of the dance floor.

She was stiff and furious, the hand he held in his a fist, but he didn't let go.

"Let me explain," he said. A low, desperate growl. "Please."

"No need." Her beautiful eyes were so dark as she gazed steadily back at him. "I understood all of that just fine."

"Zara—"

"You should have told me," she said, cutting him off, her voice less brittle but far more fierce. "There was no reason in the world you should have dropped that on me."

But, of course, that had been deliberate, too. Because she wasn't her sister. Because every emotion she ever had was written across her pretty face in all those shades of red. Her shock. Her humiliation when he asked the question, telling the truth before she said a word. Because she was obviously not the kind of woman who played the sorts of games everyone else in that room did.

"I see," she said when he said nothing, and she sounded beaten then. Lost.

Chase tightened his hand at the small of her back, and he forgot where they were. He forgot everything but Zara. His beautiful, noble Zara, who he'd ruined the way he ruined everything. Just as he'd told her he would do.

"I love you," he said because there was nothing else to say but that, no defense he could possibly offer, and she jerked as if he'd hit her. "And I warned you this would happen. This is what I do, Zara. I ruin everything I touch."

"We both live in the past," she said, harsh and low. "It's all we see. Your mother, my father. The horrible things my sister told me when I was a teenager. My grandmother, who already died. It's nothing but darkness. It's corrosive and blinding. It's a festering swamp."

Around them, people were chanting, and Chase realized that he and Zara had stopped moving.

"It's over now," he said. "It's done. This is the future. Here. Tonight."

"It's never over," she whispered. "It's never done. It goes on. It always goes on. It feeds on itself and consumes everything in its path. You know that as well as I do. You used it to your advantage in that boardroom."

"That part of it is over," he promised her. "There's only you and me now, and we—"

"There is no *we*," Zara said, very distinctive despite the clamor all around them, and despite the tears he saw well up in her eyes, making his chest feel so tight it was like some kind of pneumonia. "I like my Gothic terrors in books. I want to be able to trust the people in my life, not worry about the things they might be plotting. I want to be able to love the man who claims he loves me without worrying about his ulterior motives. I want better than this mess."

"Zara—"

"I want better than a man who would sell me out, Chase," she said, cutting him off as the first tear fell. "No matter why he did it."

Then the band started playing and the crowd cheered. The new year had begun, and Chase was nothing but a ghost, like the ones that had haunted him all this time. Zara had brought him back to life. And he'd killed that, too.

"Please," he said. "Don't go. Not like this."

But she only shook her head, her lips pressed tight together. Then she pulled out of his grip, and he had no choice but to let her do it. No choice in any of this, because this was his doing. Streamers and balloons poured down from above, there was kissing and singing and all the usual jubilation, and long after the crowd swallowed her up, long after she'd disappeared into the night, Chase still stood there.

He stood there a long time. Long after she'd left him. Long after the singing had turned to harder, drunker partying. Like if he stood there long enough, if he kept his vigil, it might bring her back.

When he knew the truth was, nothing could.

Zara saw the headlights flash through the windows of her cottage, interrupting the Jane Austen comfort reading she'd been doing on her very deep and comfortable chaise in front of the fire. She lifted up her head and frowned out toward the dark January night, wondering if someone had missed the turnoff for the public beach and found their way down her private lane instead—something that happened more often in the summertime.

She heard the slam of a car door and then, moments later, heavy steps on her front porch. Then a brusque, confident hand against the thick, old, sturdy New England wood of her front door. Zara didn't move. She stayed where she was, tucked up under a throw, scowling at the door. Maybe if she didn't make a single sound—

"I know you're in there, Zara," Chase said, loud enough that she could hear both that low rasp of his voice and the dark exasperation that colored it. "If not, I'll have to ring the fire department, as your chimney appears to be on fire."

She found she was up and on her feet without meaning to move, and she had no idea how that happened. Or how she found herself across the room with her hand on the doorknob. She caught herself there.

It had been four days since she'd last seen Chase. Since she'd turned and left him on that dance floor, unsure even now how she'd managed to walk at all when she'd been irreparably damaged by what had happened in that board-room. And the truth was, she was still such a fool where he was concerned. She knew it. She could feel her body readying itself for him, as if nothing had happened. Even her idiotic heart beat harder, as if he'd never broken it so deliberately. So cruelly.

"Zara." His voice was so dark, so close. "I can say I'm sorry through the door, but it isn't the same, is it?"

She didn't mean to open the damned thing, but she did. And then he was standing there, right there in front of her. The porch light cast him in whites and golds, but that did nothing to mute the effect of those eyes of his that skew-ered her and made her ache immediately. He looked tired, she thought, though she hated herself for noticing. Tired and drawn, but then again, he was Chase Whitaker. Even his worst was remarkably beautiful.

And that terrible song that was him, only him, swelled inside of her.

"The door's open," Zara said as evenly as she could. "Apologize away."

His gorgeous mouth tilted up in one corner, and those wild, perfectly blue eyes lit with the sort of ruefulness she wished she could share. "Is this the part where I grovel, Zara? Is that what it will take?"

"That all depends on whether or not you feel you have reason to grovel," she retorted. She leaned against the door frame and pretended she didn't feel the icy blast of the wind that swept in from Long Island Sound and cut straight through her. She told herself it might keep her focused— less susceptible to him, somehow. "And that is between you and whatever passes for your conscience."

Chase's gaze darkened, but he nodded. "I deserve that."

This was worse, Zara decided. This was worse than what she'd been doing the past few days, which was figuring out the best coping mechanisms for living with a broken heart and the ghost of this man she seemed to cart around with her wherever she went.

Much worse.

"I already told you we don't need to do this," she said then. "I don't want to look back anymore. I'm finished."

She meant that. She'd said the same thing to her father and Ariella when they'd tracked her down here on New Year's Day, after she'd failed to respond to the approximately thirty-five thousand texts and voice mail messages they'd left her, all predictably abusive.

She'd opened the door to them, too. And she'd let them storm inside. Ariella had lounged about on the couch while her father had raged. It had gone on and on. Zara had simply stood in front of the fire and watched them both, wondering how she'd ever fooled herself into thinking there was anything there that could be saved. Or why she'd tried so hard to do the saving. *You're the only reason I tried, Grams*, she'd thought. *But no more.*

When her father had wound down, she'd smiled. Not, she'd imagined, a very nice smile.

"Okay," she'd said calmly. "I heard you. Now, please leave."

They'd both stared back at her.

"I don't think you understand the gravity of this situation," Amos had seethed at her. "I sank ten years of my life into Whitaker Industries and you handed it over to the enemy—"

"It's you who doesn't understand," she'd replied, cutting him off, which she knew happened rarely. "The only reason you're here is because you think I can do something for you. The only reason Ariella is here is because she feeds off cruelty. Neither of those reasons have anything to do with me."

"This is about our family," Amos had snapped at her.

"What family is that?" Zara had asked, and she'd known

she was doing the right thing, however overdue, because she felt nothing. No upset, no victory. Just an emptiness and her solid, bone-deep conviction that this had to end. "I'd love to have a family. My desire for one is what allowed all of this to happen. My loyalty to Grams, who you hated and Ariella ignored. But she's dead, and I shouldn't have to prove myself worthy of love you never give anyway."

"So melodramatic," Ariella had murmured. "This is about what happened at The Plaza, isn't it?"

"I used to hero-worship you, Ariella," Zara had said quietly. "Now I don't even know who you are."

Ariella had rolled her eyes, but Zara had thought that the lack of a toxic reply might have meant she'd hit a nerve. But that, too, hadn't mattered any longer.

"You listen to me, Zara," Amos had begun to say, all bluster and volume.

"No," she'd said very distinctly, and maybe it was the utter lack of fear she felt showing through on her face. She didn't know, but Amos subsided. "You listen to me for a change. We are done. If you want to regain your place at Whitaker Industries, you can figure that out on your own. I'm officially not interested."

"Are you choosing a man who would throw you to the wolves over your own family?" he'd asked as if astounded.

"Where do you think I learned how to survive being thrown to the wolves, Dad?" she'd asked coolly. "What Chase did felt like a warm bath in comparison."

"You'll regret this," Amos had promised her.

"No," she'd replied as they'd gathered their coats and stormed toward the door. "I won't. But if either of you ever do, you know where to find me."

The slam of her front door had sounded a lot like finality. But it had also sounded like freedom. She'd decided she welcomed both.

And now she stood before yet another wolf, and this time, she couldn't pretend that she was empty. She couldn't pretend she felt nothing. But she didn't want to let him in, either.

"You might be finished," Chase said now, his dark blue eyes searching hers. "But I'm in love with you."

Zara wanted to slam the door in his face, but she didn't. She turned abruptly and walked back toward the fire, fighting to keep all the things she felt from her face. She heard Chase step inside and close the door behind him.

"I knew there was no way I could get out of marrying your sister," he said without preamble. Zara scowled at the dancing flames in front of her and told herself she didn't want to hear this. But she didn't say anything that might stop him, either. "Your father had worked it all perfectly. I was vulnerable. The deal with Nicodemus was set to go through, but that only meant the company would be more powerful. Amos could still fire me from my own family legacy. And it's all I had left. It's all Mattie and I had of our father. It was the thing he loved most, save my mother."

She didn't want to melt. She didn't want to feel anything at all. She didn't want to imagine a terrified thirteen-year-old boy and how brave he must have been to try to save his sister on the side of that long-ago road, to stay quiet while he couldn't save his mother.

"And I believed I'd killed her," Chase said quietly. "I knew I had. It never occurred to me that there could be another way of looking at what happened. I'm still not sure there is, but thanks to you, there's doubt. There's the possibility that I'm not the murderer I've always known I was. But none of that was even a glimmer of possibility on any horizon a month ago, as I was set to marry Ariella."

Zara folded her arms over her middle and turned around then. She had to swallow hard. Chase stood just inside the door, still wearing his coat, ice and wet clinging to his black hair. He was all in black, except those eyes of his, and they were the clearest she'd ever seen them. No ghosts. No lonely seas. Just all that deep, dark blue. And he was looking at her like he never wanted to look at anything else again.

She had to bite her own lip hard to keep from going to him.

"I'd met your sister before. I'd certainly read about her." His mouth moved into something like a smile. "I've met a thousand women just like your sister, and I knew what I was getting into with her. It made it easy to come up with a perfect plan. But then you turned up. You looked ridiculous in that dress, and yet still, you were *you*. Zara. Undiminished by the dress, the wedding itself, your father. Like none of his dirt could touch you at all. You rose above it."

"That's absurd, revisionist history," she snapped, before she could think better of it. "You were drunk."

"Then you stood up in that bathtub," he said, his voice going hoarse. "And you brought me back to life, Zara. In that instant. But I'd set a course. I had a plan. And it had never occurred to me to factor in emotions. I wasn't capable of any, I thought, and certainly your sister isn't. But how could I have planned for you?" His mouth crooked again when she only stared back at him, stricken. "I can't imagine that anyone could spend any kind of time with you and *not* fall in love with you. I can't. I didn't."

"This isn't love, Chase." She ignored the wild cartwheels of her heart, her stomach. "This is guilt."

"I haven't felt anything but guilt in twenty years," he threw back at her. "I know the difference."

She shook her head hard.

"It's too late," she said quickly before she second-guessed herself. "I gave you everything I had and you chose to waste it by using me as a pawn in your little battle with my father."

"I regret using you," he said. His gaze slammed into hers. "But you hardly gave me 'everything,' Zara. You only told me that you might have loved me, that you wished you could have done, when you were leaving me."

"Was that the time to declare my love? Right after you'd showed me that yet again, the only time anyone pretends any interest in me at all is when they need me for their own ends?"

"You're making my point for me."

"I am doing no such thing," she snapped at him, and she didn't realize she'd advanced on him until his hands came up to grip her shoulders, and then it was too late. "I spent twenty-six years trying to work things out with my father. I'm not going to waste another day playing the same kind of games with a man who's just like him."

"Zara." Chase's voice was like gravel. "I'm not your bloody father."

"Tell me what the difference is!" she raged at him. She didn't realize her hands had curled into fists until she thumped them on his chest. "Tell me how I'm supposed to tell you apart! You both do nothing but use me, tell me whatever lies you think might make me do what you want, never giving one thought to what *I* might need!"

"The difference is, I'm here." His voice was low and commanding at once, and it cut through the storm in her, beating it back. He shifted, running his thumbs below her eyes to clear away a wetness she hadn't even known was there, and her heart clutched in her chest. "The difference is, I'm not going anywhere. I can't live without you, Zara. I don't want to try. The house is too big, the bed keeps me awake and it *hurts*. I don't care what it takes, I'll do it. Just come back to me. Let me prove that whatever happened over the past month, whatever happened at that damned party, *this marriage* is the one good thing to come of it."

She pulled back from him then, though she couldn't seem to step away, almost as if her bones had melted and she was stuck right there.

"You're not meant for someone like me," she told him, and he would never know how hard that was for her to admit. "I know that. If you don't know it now, you will. I'm sure the relentlessly negative attention from all those tabloids that adore my sister and yours will help."

Chase studied her for one of those too-long moments.

"This is what I'm talking about," he murmured. "Who gives a toss what the tabloids say? They're a soap opera— this is life. And you've spent much too long listening to petty comments from the likes of your sister."

"And yet, at the end of the day, you're the one who used me," she said quietly.

"Just as you used me, Zara," he pointed out gently. "To work out your Daddy issues. The only difference is that what I did was successful."

She scowled at him then, and he sighed.

"I have an idea," he said. "Let's decide that the rest of this marriage is ours. Just ours, starting now. No outside voices or influences need apply." His gorgeous eyes bored into hers. "Because they don't matter. They never will."

And she wanted to fall forward and trust that he'd catch her. She wanted to believe him this time. God, how she wanted that. But she shook her head again and moved back a step, because the truth was, imagination never got her into anything but trouble. Her heart was a liar. And if she didn't protect herself now, who would?

Chase reached over and took her hands in his, and then he dropped down before her. Onto one knee. Zara blinked. Then realized she'd stopped breathing.

"What are you doing?" she managed to ask, almost soundlessly.

"Zara Elliott," he intoned, and his eyes were the blue of summer skies, with only the faintest hint of shadows to mar them. "You've already married me. But I want you to be my wife. I want you to honor the vows you made to me when I was a stranger, and I want to dedicate myself to honoring the same vows I made when I'd had a little too much whiskey. I want to spend years sleeping in the same bed with you and waking there, too. I want to build a life from all the little pieces we stitched together in this past month. I want you to tell me stories, and I want to make more of our own. I want you to teach me how to love Christmas the way you do. I want to love you so well and so deeply that when you look back, you'll forget you ever doubted I could."

And Zara stopped fighting. She stopped trying to ward him off when he was the one thing she wanted, so desperately it actually made her shake. She couldn't help the tears that coursed down her cheeks then. She knelt before him, pulling her hands from his to hold his face. His beautiful face, and the far more complicated and fascinated man behind it.

"Chase," she whispered. "I do love you. I do."

"I know you do," he whispered back, *fierce and certain and hers*, she thought. *Finally hers.* "And we have all the time in the world to prove it."

And Zara would never know who moved first, but then they were kissing. Again and again, as if that was the only truth that mattered. That beautiful fire that was only theirs. That wild bright light that burned in both of them.

And would keep on burning, she thought then—holding him close, this man who had been her husband before he became the love of her life—forever.

Christmas Day, one year later...

"This has a certain, horrifying symmetry," Mattie said as she stood by the window in their father's office at Green-leigh that Chase had long since claimed as his own. "But if you order me to marry someone else, Nicodemus will have a fit."

Chase grinned, imagining the reaction his brother-in-law—a man he was beginning to consider a friend, even a good one—might have. One similar to his own, were any-one to suggest he marry someone other than Zara.

His Zara, who he loved more now than he'd ever imag-ined he could love anyone. He thought it grew by the day, making his shriveled old heart expand every time she smiled at him. And she smiled at him quite a lot.

She'd insisted they celebrate Christmas this year, and so they were. Dutifully, Chase had thought, at least on his part—but it was impossible not to succumb to the infec-tiousness of Zara's pure, unadulterated joy. That was true whether the subject was a book, a holiday or life itself. It had been her determination to reach out to Mattie that had created the bridge between Chase and his sister that, in his guilt, he'd never known how to build.

"Of course we're inviting them for Christmas dinner," Zara had said, and as she'd been naked at the time and moving her hips against his in a way designed to make him her slave, he'd agreed.

Though secretly, Chase knew he would have agreed anyway. Especially now that the family lawyer had pro-duced that letter.

"Are you ready?" he asked Mattie.

She turned and looked at him, her expression serious. "How can I answer that? Is anyone ever ready for a mes-sage from beyond the grave?"

The letter was from Big Bart, their attorney had told

Chase when he'd delivered this letter only yesterday. And their father had left very specific instructions about when and how it was to be opened.

When they're both happy, were the words on the envelope.

"Apparently, the Calloways are the informants," Chase said now. "We've been deemed happy." He swallowed. "Is that right?"

Mattie blinked. Then smiled.

"Yes," she said softly. "I'm happy. You did a good thing, Chase. The truth is, I wish I'd married Nicodemus a long time ago."

It was another great weight from his back. He nodded. Then he held up the envelope. Mattie inclined her head, indicating that she was ready. Chase thrust his thumb beneath the sealed flap, opening it and pulling two sheets of paper forth, both written on in pen in Big Bart's distinctive hand. Mattie came to stand next to him, and with another glance at each other, they began to read.

My dearest Chase and Mattie

If you are reading this letter, I am no longer with you and more than that, I left you the same coward I've been all these years.

The facts aren't pretty. Your mother's death was no one's fault but mine. She warned me a thousand times not to cross certain lines, but I didn't listen. I was Big Bart Whitaker. I knew best. Those gunmen were after me, not her—

"Gunmen?" Mattie asked in a horrified whisper.

"I'll tell you everything I know," Chase promised, his throat raw. "In a minute."

Mattie's eyes were too bright, but she nodded. And Chase felt better than he would have admitted a year ago when she moved even closer, like he really was the big brother he knew he'd never been to her. Maybe this was a new start, too.

—and I've never forgiven myself for not being there. For letting my sins catch up to the people I love most. I wish I could have told you both all of this. I wish I knew how. I wish I'd been the father you deserved, but the only way I knew how to be that man was with your mother's help. Without her, I fear I was nothing but a blowhard. Lost and no good to anyone.

I know you've both blamed yourself for that day in your own ways. I hope that this letter finds you truly happy, as you deserve to be. As your mother would have insisted you be. And I want you to know that while I couldn't save her or protect you from living through the terror of it, I could and did find the men responsible and make certain they, at least, paid for their crimes. I imagine the great hereafter is where I'll pay for mine.

But you, Chase and Mattie, have paid more than enough. My beautiful children. I couldn't be more proud of either one of you. I wish I'd been man enough to let you know that when it mattered the most.

Live. Love. Let the past lie where it should.

Be happy. I know you'll be better—you already are.

Dad

And when they finally emerged from the study, Chase felt like a different man. Weightless. Washed clean. He'd told Mattie everything he knew. They'd talked about their memories, their guilt. Their shared dismay over the distance in their relationship. Mattie wasn't the only one to grow a bit misty-eyed.

As they walked down the great stairs of Greenleigh together, Chase was sure he could feel all the usual ghosts around them. But this time, there was nothing but joy. And, finally, hope.

A great, bright future instead of the terrible past.

As they walked into the kitchens, they could see Zara sitting up on one of the counters, talking with great animation to Nicodemus, who looked as ferocious as ever, even as he listened closely to whatever it was she was saying. Zara waved her hands about, the light catching the rings she wore on her left hand—two that Chase had put there the day he'd married her, and the pretty band of yellow diamonds that reminded him of her eyes when she was happy, that he'd put there a month later. When he'd been able to admit he was in love with her.

Mattie laughed beside him, a sound that reminded him of the happy girl she'd been the last time he'd heard it. "What do you think they're talking about?"

"With Zara?" Chase grinned as Zara looked over and caught his eye, and her broad smile was still like sunshine, even inside. Even when she taught him every day how deeply he could love, and how fiercely she could love in return. How beautiful all of this was, if they were together. "It could be anything. Let's hope it's not the story of her bloody lost kitten."

Because that particular story was his.

And the truth was, Chase really had been terrified of the one thing he'd wanted most, and Zara had saved him, too.

* * * * *

Mills & Boon® Hardback
December 2014

ROMANCE

Taken Over by the Billionaire	Miranda Lee
Christmas in Da Conti's Bed	Sharon Kendrick
His for Revenge	Caitlin Crews
A Rule Worth Breaking	Maggie Cox
What The Greek Wants Most	Maya Blake
The Magnate's Manifesto	Jennifer Hayward
To Claim His Heir by Christmas	Victoria Parker
Heiress's Defiance	Lynn Raye Harris
Nine Month Countdown	Leah Ashton
Bridesmaid with Attitude	Christy McKellen
An Offer She Can't Refuse	Shoma Narayanan
Breaking the Boss's Rules	Nina Milne
Snowbound Surprise for the Billionaire	Michelle Douglas
Christmas Where They Belong	Marion Lennox
Meet Me Under the Mistletoe	Cara Colter
A Diamond in Her Stocking	Kandy Shepherd
Falling for Dr December	Susanne Hampton
Snowbound with the Surgeon	Annie Claydon

MEDICAL

Midwife's Christmas Proposal	Fiona McArthur
Midwife's Mistletoe Baby	Fiona McArthur
A Baby on Her Christmas List	Louisa George
A Family This Christmas	Sue MacKay

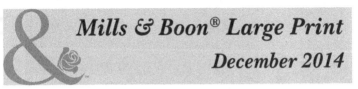

ROMANCE

Zarif's Convenient Queen	Lynne Graham
Uncovering Her Nine Month Secret	Jennie Lucas
His Forbidden Diamond	Susan Stephens
Undone by the Sultan's Touch	Caitlin Crews
The Argentinian's Demand	Cathy Williams
Taming the Notorious Sicilian	Michelle Smart
The Ultimate Seduction	Dani Collins
The Rebel and the Heiress	Michelle Douglas
Not Just a Convenient Marriage	Lucy Gordon
A Groom Worth Waiting For	Sophie Pembroke
Crown Prince, Pregnant Bride	Kate Hardy

HISTORICAL

Beguiled by Her Betrayer	Louise Allen
The Rake's Ruined Lady	Mary Brendan
The Viscount's Frozen Heart	Elizabeth Beacon
Mary and the Marquis	Janice Preston
Templar Knight, Forbidden Bride	Lynna Banning

MEDICAL

200 Harley Street: The Soldier Prince	Kate Hardy
200 Harley Street: The Enigmatic Surgeon	Annie Claydon
A Father for Her Baby	Sue MacKay
The Midwife's Son	Sue MacKay
Back in Her Husband's Arms	Susanne Hampton
Wedding at Sunday Creek	Leah Martyn

Mills & Boon® Hardback
January 2015

ROMANCE

The Secret His Mistress Carried	Lynne Graham
Nine Months to Redeem Him	Jennie Lucas
Fonseca's Fury	Abby Green
The Russian's Ultimatum	Michelle Smart
To Sin with the Tycoon	Cathy Williams
The Last Heir of Monterrato	Andie Brock
Inherited by Her Enemy	Sara Craven
Sheikh's Desert Duty	Maisey Yates
The Honeymoon Arrangement	Joss Wood
Who's Calling the Shots?	Jennifer Rae
The Scandal Behind the Wedding	Bella Frances
The Bridegroom Wishlist	Tanya Wright
Taming the French Tycoon	Rebecca Winters
His Very Convenient Bride	Sophie Pembroke
The Heir's Unexpected Return	Jackie Braun
The Prince She Never Forgot	Scarlet Wilson
A Child to Bind Them	Lucy Clark
The Baby That Changed Her Life	Louisa Heaton

MEDICAL

How to Find a Man in Five Dates	Tina Beckett
Breaking Her No-Dating Rule	Amalie Berlin
It Happened One Night Shift	Amy Andrews
Tamed by Her Army Doc's Touch	Lucy Ryder

1214GEN STD HB

Mills & Boon® Large Print
January 2015

ROMANCE

The Housekeeper's Awakening	Sharon Kendrick
More Precious than a Crown	Carol Marinelli
Captured by the Sheikh	Kate Hewitt
A Night in the Prince's Bed	Chantelle Shaw
Damaso Claims His Heir	Annie West
Changing Constantinou's Game	Jennifer Hayward
The Ultimate Revenge	Victoria Parker
Interview with a Tycoon	Cara Colter
Her Boss by Arrangement	Teresa Carpenter
In Her Rival's Arms	Alison Roberts
Frozen Heart, Melting Kiss	Ellie Darkins

HISTORICAL

Lord Havelock's List	Annie Burrows
The Gentleman Rogue	Margaret McPhee
Never Trust a Rebel	Sarah Mallory
Saved by the Viking Warrior	Michelle Styles
The Pirate Hunter	Laura Martin

MEDICAL

200 Harley Street: The Shameless Maverick	Louisa George
200 Harley Street: The Tortured Hero	Amy Andrews
A Home for the Hot-Shot Doc	Dianne Drake
A Doctor's Confession	Dianne Drake
The Accidental Daddy	Meredith Webber
Pregnant with the Soldier's Son	Amy Ruttan

MILLS & BOON®

Why shop at millsandboon.co.uk?

Each year, thousands of romance readers find their perfect read at millsandboon.co.uk. That's because we're passionate about bringing you the very best romantic fiction. Here are some of the advantages of shopping at www.millsandboon.co.uk:

* **Get new books first**—you'll be able to buy your favourite books one month before they hit the shops

* **Get exclusive discounts**—you'll also be able to buy our specially created monthly collections, with up to 50% off the RRP

* **Find your favourite authors**—latest news, interviews and new releases for all your favourite authors and series on our website, plus ideas for what to try next

* **Join in**—once you've bought your favourite books, don't forget to register with us to rate, review and join in the discussions

Visit **www.millsandboon.co.uk**
for all this and more today!